Isle of the Beast

By

J. WESLEY BUCK

ISLE OF THE BEAST

Prologue

Report sent to the Committee on Deep Space Exploration and Alien Civilizations.

Re: Planet Ephus   Date of Discovery: 6/7/2442 ship time. First Contact: No contact has been attempted. This report is a review of the circumstances leading to this decision. All of the following events were observed and recorded by United Systems Cruiser Magellan, using sensors and special scanners. The language of the planet is as close to Earth equivalent as possible as well as the computer-translator was able to interpret it.

Civilization on Epheus is primitive compared to Earth. The intelligent groups on Ephus are similar to Orangutans and Chimpanzees, with a related group of Gorillas that live in a state comparable to South Pacific natives, circa 1880-1940 C.E.

There are also tribes of primitive proto-humans on a small continent in Epheus' Eastern Hemisphere. The Simian civilization has made no attempt to colonize or govern that continent. The proto-humans lack any sense of intelligent motivation.

The civilization is remarkably like pre-mid-twentieth century Earth with one striking exception; the Simians have not developed flight. They have developed radio communication. Their government is unified, except for the continent mentioned above and islands that lay far from the main continents.

It is a society based on an exclusive, but not rigid, caste system. Simians can move to a higher caste by diligent effort and prestigious work. The distinction between castes is as follows: the lowest use only their given names.

The suffix –Um distinguishes the next higher caste, followed by –Us. The highest caste has –Uy. While females can attain admission to a higher caste they retain only –A.

It is recommended by the commanding officer that any contact with the Simians be delayed until they have achieved a higher level of technological development. It is the considered opinion of the ship's staff that the planet Epheus be kept under periodic surveillance. It is hoped the council will seriously consider these recommendations.

With this background, here is the full report as it has been monitored from the planet. The report has been transcribed to discs for the convenience of the Committee, and other associated authorities, That may become involved. Produced under the supervision of Alfred M. Highland, Communications Chief, Cruiser Magellan. Note: words followed by (?) are approximations not literal translations.

THE EXPEDITION

Dr. Sey-Us stood lost in thought, staring out the rain-splattered window at the dark glistening stone and concrete skyscrapers. They tapered like obscure obliska into an opaque sky filled with bulging, scudding gray clouds precipitating misty drizzle. He turned to his desk where the only light in the room reflected from the polished surface. The office was engulfed in gloomy semidarkness, broken only by the steady glow of the brass desk lamp. In the area of light lay a green-edged telegram and a battered, taped map.

As if pulled by a magnet, his eyes were drawn to the documents. The map was of Scumm Island, yellowed, taped, and hand drawn. Sey-Us had bought the map two years ago from a Chimp captain who had just returned from a voyage in the Popus Sea. The captain had been lucky to have gotten a first hand description from a native of the Forgotten Zone. It was an area where life was cheap and death swift and violent. The Forgotten Zone abounded in island legends and myths from ancient times.

The captain had met Sey-Us at the port of Icense after his return from the Institute's North Polar Expedition. It had been with the hope that Sey-Us would be interested in the map that the Chimp had approached him. It was the first factual evidence Sey-Us had discovered of Scumm Island. He had already heard of the strange beast that lived on the island before ever laying eyes on the map. Sey-Us had purchased the map for a modest sum.

What the captain had told him came to intrigue him more and more, and he set about to search for further proof of the island. He hadn't found anything factual but a wealth of detail in legend. What he had found led him to believe the story the captain had told him was truthful.

Now, two years later, his research had uncovered all the available evidence – calling it evidence was stretching the truth. His opportunity was now at hand. Sey-Us thought of what it would mean to capture the great beast of legend and return it alive. To bring Gnok back no matter what it turned out to be would be quite an achievement. Sey-Us was also determined to discover whatever other mysteries Scumm Island might hold.

Sey-Us held his age good, actually looking ten years younger than his true forty-six, and not a gray fur on his body. He made sure to keep in good physical shape knowing expeditions could prove taxing on the body as well as the mind.

He went to the desk and sat down, his hand reaching for the welcome, but not unexpected, telegram he had received earlier. Once more he let his eyes wander over the sentences as if they contained some cosmic secret. Sey-Us could hardly believe what he held before his brown eyes.

TO: DR. SEY-US. ANTHROPOLOGICAL INSTITUTE, SIMALIA
FROM: DR. CARI-US, PLANETARY INSTITUTE FOR THE STUDY OF ANTHRPOLOGY AND PRIMIVE CULTURE, LIPUR
THIS IS TO INFORM YOU THAT YOUR REQUEST FOR FUNDS FOR AN EXPEDITION TO A NUMBER OF ISLANDS IN THE POPUS AND OI SEAS AREA IS HEARBY APPROVED. STOP. YOUR SELECT PARTY TO DEPART WITHIN THIRTY (30) DAYS. STOP. THE RESEARCH VESSEL NO'MO IS AT YOUR SERVICE. STOP. EXPECT WEEKLY REPORTS OF PROGRESS. STOP. GOOD LUCK. END.
YOUR ESTEEMED COLLEAGUE, DR. CARI-US

Sey-Us turned his eyes up to the dark ceiling. Thirty days! Everything would have to be moved south to Icense, the port where the No'mo was permanently berthed. He would have to start on the paperwork and delivery schedules tomorrow. He was abruptly startled from his thoughts by a rapping on the door.

"Enter," Sey-Us said, in an alert tone. It was his young aides, who had just returned from their honeymoon. Gonail-Um was the most promising protégé he had ever had the pleasure of teaching and working with at the University. Odeer-A, his lovely wife, also possessed an exceptional intellect and quick biting wit.

"We received your message and came right over, Dr. Sey-Us," Gonail-Um said, expectantly.

"Please turn on the overhead light and be seated," Sey-Us said. "This is a momentous occasion in the history of anthropology." Odeer-A and Gonail-Um exchanged wondering looks as they took seats in front of their huge desk. They sat silent for a long moment as Sey-Us rubbed his eyes and put his thoughts in order. He put his arms on the desk and regarded them with a twinkle in his eyes.

"How would you like a second honeymoon? A working one, to be sure. My expedition has been approved. We're going to the Popus and Oi Seas." Sey-Us knew their answer having worked and taught them for over three years.

"You know you can count on us, Dr. Sey-Us," Odeer-A said, glancing at Gonail-Um, to be certain he agreed.

"We would be honored to accompany you on your expedition," Gonail-Um said. Sey-Us hesitated to tell them the whole story, although he knew they could be trusted above anyone else.

Sey-Us made up his mind. If he wanted their help then they deserved the truth – at least, most of it. What part of what he believed should he tell them?

"What I'm about to tell you must, at this time, go no further than this office," Sey-Us said, in a serious tone. "Do I have your word to keep silent?"

"Unreservedly, as you well know, Dr. Sey-Us," Gonail-Um replied. "We would never betray your confidence in us." Odeer-A looked at her husband with a puzzled expression. This wasn't like the Dr. Sey-Us they knew and respected. In the time they had worked with him he had never been secretive.

"We're your personal aides, sir," Odeer-A said, sincerely. "We're loyal to you. Why are you suddenly questioning our trust?" Sey-Us held up a hand.

"It's not that I don't trust you," he said, knowing he couldn't deny both felt deeply the words they had spoken. Yet he hesitated. Sey-Us didn't want to give them the impression he was chasing a pipe dream. He had to tell them the factual parts of his research. They deserved that much consideration.

"Have either of you heard of Scumm Island?"

"Not until now," Odeer-A replied. Gonail-Um thought for a moment before replying.

"I seem to vaguely recall some reference to it, Dr. Sey-Us. Isn't it a legendary place?" Gonail-Um quickly raised a hand.

"Wait a moment. Isn't it an island in the Forgotten Zone where some sort of legendary beast is alleged to exist? Is that where we're going?" Sey-Us saw the excitement growing in Gonail-Um. He didn't reply, just held out the map and telegram to them.

A gasp escaped Odeer-A when she saw the map and a bright twinkle of adventure came to Gonail-Um's eyes. They looked over the map and telegram in silence. They glanced at each other and Gonail-Um handed the papers back. Their thoughts were coming too fast to put in words.

After a few minutes of contemplation, they were certain about their decision to go.

"Are you certain the map is authentic, Dr. Sey-Us?" Gonail-um asked, in a humble tone. "I mean, considering it is hand drawn, it would draw suspicion. I mean no disrespect by the question, sir." Sey-Us sternly tapped a finger on the desk.

"It's much too detailed to be a fake," he replied. "And from what I've been able to learn from two years of research, I'm positive it's an exact representation of Scumm Island. It does lie in the Forgotten Zone, as you said. Now, with a fully funded expedition, I shall find it and prove its existence beyond doubt."

"What is it about that particular island that fires your interest so intensely, Doctor?" Odeer-A asked. That was the question he had been expecting to hear from Gonail-Um. Sey-Us thought about how much alike they were.

"Because I have no idea what we may discover there. And that alone is enough to whet my curiosity. It should be the same for you both – if you've the salt of a good scientist in your mind."

"Surely you must have some idea of what's there, sir," Gonail-Um said, hoping to get Sey-Us to tell more about what his research had revealed. But Sey-Us wasn't opening up just yet.

"I have only legends about what may be on that island, and those can be read from any book on the Forgotten Zone. I intend to thoroughly investigate that island. But it will be you two I'll be depending on to aid me in unlocking its secrets." Sey-Us leaned back and regarded them for a moment.

"Who knows what we might find?" he asked, with a mysterious look.

"I must say I'm impressed, Dr. Sey-Us," Odeer-A said. "How did you convince Dr. Cari-Us to back your request for funds? And get it approved. That's all the more remarkable when one considers his penny-pinching attitude."

"Odeer-A!" Gonail-Um exclaimed. Sey-Us looked at her.

"I'm surprised at a remark like that about one our esteemed colleagues," Sey-Us said, feigning shock. "Although I must admit there's more than a grain of truth in what you say. He made me wait over a year before recommending approval. He gave my plan very careful consideration and me an irritating delay." Gonail-Um scratched his jaw looking thoughtful.

"Since we're committed to start in thirty days, aren't we going to be in a flutter getting the equipment shipped to Icense and stowed aboard the No'mo?" Odeer-A asked.

"Flaming hell! To get the equipment moved, we're going to have to bust ass," Sey-Us replied. "Excuse my anatomy, Odeer-A."

"That's putting it mildly, sir," Gonail-Um said, shaking his head at the thought of paperwork. He began figuring how many trucks would be needed since he would have the responsibility for the transfer. The main thought in his mind was what a trip it would be. Adventure, danger, excitement, pure Sey-Us grist for his hard mill.

"Will we be taking firearms and the new vapor bombs?" Gonail-Um asked. "If so, they will require special handlers." Odeer-A gave Sey-Us a surprised look.

"Is it necessary to go armed?" she asked, concerned at what that implied and the danger it would entail. Sey-Us and Gonail-Um turned their eyes to her, expressing disbelief at her naivety of the Forgotten Zone.

"My dear, I'm surprised you would ask such a question," Sey-Us said, in a reasonable tone. "The arms are for our protection. Savage tribes of Gorillas inhabit those islands and are cannibals and headhunters. Then there's the unknown beats we may have to face." She raised her hand to her lips.

"Oh, my! That does put some poop in the picture. Are you certain the Gorillas would present a threat to us?"

"Most certainly," Gohail-Um replied. Sey-Us stood and regarded them for a moment.

"You have three days to get your affairs in order," he said. "Then report to the ship. I'll need you there to make certain everything is stowed in the order we'll' need it. Captain Mai-Us is to be told nothing about our destination. I'll' inform him after we sail. It's 'important that our security remain intact. I don't want Cari-Us getting any word of our planned destination." Gonail-Um was thinking ahead and decided to see if his boss would confirm what he now suspected.

"Those savages and wild beasts, are they the only reason for arming ourselves, Dr. Sey-Us?" Gonail-Um was leaning forward in an expectant pose. Sey-Us still hesitated, then decided to tell them what he was really going after since Gonail-Um had mentioned the legendary beast.

"I believe – and this is only conjecture, mind you – that there's a beast on Scumm Island. An awesome creature called Gnok. If it exists, it must be horrible beyond comprehension. I have no idea what this thing is like. But one thing is certain, for many years, this Gnok has held that island's natives in a grip of cold terror."

ICENSE

The port of Icense stood in marked contrast to Simalia. The sky was a clear orange with a few puffy clouds drifting across the face of the sun. Sey-Us had made certain the loading of equipment onboard the No'mo was completed two days ahead of their scheduled sailing date.

Sey-Us was studying a map when the captain came on the bridge. With a grim expression, he handed Sey-Us the message that had just been received by radio. Sey-Us unfolded it and read.

TO: DR. SEY-US, EXPEDITION DIRECTOR PORT OF ICENSE, RESEARCH VESSEL NO'MO.
FROM: DR. CARI-US, DIRECTOR, PLANETARY INSTITUTE
FOR THE STUDY OF ANTHROPOLOGY AND PRIMITIVE CULTURES, LIPUR.
RE: IMMEDIATE RECALL TO SAMALIA OF AIDES, GONAIL-UM AND ODEER-A. STOP. NEEDED AT UNIVERSITY AS INSTRUCTORS DUE TO YOUR PROTRACTED ABSENCE. STOP. CONTACT DR. HISTOR-US, ICENSE BRANCH FOR NEW AIDES. STOP. COMPLY AT ONCE. END.
SIGNED: YOUR ESTEEMED COLLEAGUE, DR. CARI-US, DIRECTOR PISAPC.

Sey-Us slowly raised his eyes from the message and regarded the captain.

"Flaming hell, Mai-Us!" he exploded. "They want me to take new aides on this expedition. Can you believe that? Aides I'm completely unfamiliar with and haven't trained." Sey-Us snorted in helpless rage.

"Send my well trained aides to the University as instructors! What nonsense."

"All you can do is comply, Sey-Us," Mai-Us said. "Cari-Us knows you have no choice." Sey-Us turned his eyes to the harbor. Someone was out to wreck his expedition before it left port, he thought. He had never faced interference like this on his other expeditions.

He looked at the captain and felt envious. Here was a crusty old salt who had spent his years at sea, Sey-Us thought. He had to put up with no such inference from anyone – except Sey-Us, on previous expeditions. Unlike common sailors, Mai-Us didn't take seriously the superstitions about the islands in the Popus Sea and Forgotten Zone.
Sey-Us realized Mai-Us had been speaking to him. Back to reality, he thought, and your aides. Sey-Us was bitter at this turn of events.

"What were you saying, Mai-Us?"

"Do you want me to summon Gonail-Um and Odeer-A to the bridge? I don't think you should delay, if we're to sail on time." Sey-Us slowly nodded.

"By all means, Mai-Us. I'll give them the bad news. They're going to be sorely disappointed." Mai-Us stepped to the side of the bridge, pressed a switch, and his voice filled the ship summoning the aides to face Sey-Us.

Odeer-A and Gonail-Um were devastated by the recall and knew the system allowed Sey-Us no choice but to send them on their way. Knowing the inevitable couldn't be long delayed, they left the No'mo in a dispondent mood.

In the fading twilight and veils of fog, the No'mo stood out as a sleek modern research vessel. But the most imaginative eye could not have discerned the unusual adventure she was about to embark on. Satisfied he had the right ship, Dr. Histor-Us ambled through the thin fog to the gangway. He was about to start up when a nearby shadow moved toward him.

"You one of the fools going on this crazy voyage?" an old sailor demanded, sternly. Histor-Us regarded him standing in a splash of light from an uncovered porthole.

"Crazy did you say?" Histor-Us asked, gazing at the old Orang. The word 'crazy' had quickly pushed up the conviction that hadn't been far from his mind. He definitely didn't like Sey-Us, and considered him an overbearing bully, regardless of his reputation as a scientist.

"What's crazy about a scientific expedition, old timer? They sail from here all the time." The Orang took a step closer and lowered his voice.

"The scientist that's running this show for one. Must think he's like a god or something awfully close to it." Histor-Us nodded.

"Are you referring to Dr. Sey-Us?"

"Aye, that's the one! A real odd one, I hear. I also heard that if he
wants to study a lion(?) he just walks up to it and tells it to look natural. Now if that's not crazy then I don't know what crazy is." Histor-Us chuckled. That wasn't much different from his opinion of the secretive expedition director. But he had never heard of Sey-Us hunting lions(?). That would be too tame for him. Historus-Us assumed this to be merely waterfront rumor and knew it was always rife with these sorts of rumors about ships.

"Sey-Us is a tough old bird, all right," he agreed. "But where did you get the idea that this particular voyage was crazy?" The Orang shook his head.

"It's no rumor, if that's what you're thinking," he said, stepping away from the circle of light. "There are some bright ones here, even if they don't have –Us in their names, say it's crazy. Take the cargo this Sey-Us stowed. Why there's stuff in the holds you wouldn't believe."

The Orang gave a furtive glance along the empty decks of the No'mo and continued.

"I saw some of it with my own eyes. The crew is twice the number a ship this size needs." He had said nothing that proved a case against Sey-Us. Histor-Us could see he was prepared to lay out a lengthy succession of empty charges. Before he could continue, a young, authoritative voice put an end to the old sailor's speech.

"You there, by the gangway. What do you want?" The old sailor had quickly faded into the shadows as suddenly as he had appeared. Histor-Us looked up toward the deck rail amid ships. Light falling from an open cabin silhouetted a figure. As the silhouette stepped into the light, Histor-Us recalled Sey-Us' description and felt it was the first mate he was looking at. The slim Orang Sey-Us had praised so highly stood in the light, his daring eyes aglow and a strong jaw.

Histor-Us was usually reserved when meeting someone. But he had an instant liking for Risc-Um. It was the commanding, steady voice that impressed him. There, he thought, is an intelligent Orang. With such an officer, the idea of the expedition being called crazy seemed ludicrous.

"Waterfront rumor be damned," Histor-Us mumbled. He felt foolish for taking the old sailor seriously.

"What is it you want?" the brisk voice demanded. Histor-Us made a quick look around but saw no trace of the old sailor. He turned back and looked up to where Risc-Um was standing.

"I wish to come on board. I must speak with Dr. Sey-Us." He became somewhat cheerful at his sudden liking for the first mate.

"Come aboard," Risc-Um said. Histor-Us began a cautious ascent up the damp, slippery gangway. Stepping on deck, he faced Risc-Um and his first close look gave him the impression of an officer who would brook no foolishness.

"If you're Histor-Us, Sey-Us has been waiting for you. He believes you're bringing him new aides." Histor-Us felt annoyance at Sey-Us' presumption.

"I am Histor-Us. But even I have limitations. As you can see my physical condition suffers from my work," he said, still breathing hard from his ascent. The mate grinned as Histor-Us got his breathing slowed.

"Welcome aboard the No'mo. I see you've come alone. That means Sey-Us will probably go through the roof." Risc-Um had no illusions as to what was about to happen. Histor-Us felt a chill at the prospect of facing an angry Sey-Us but said nothing. As Risc-Um turned, Histor-Us scowled and followed. The mate's quick, swaggering stride took them forward and up a ladder to the bridge. Risc-Um opened the door allowing Histor-Us to step in. His first impression of the bright interior was that of a clean, almost antiseptic, scene. It was furnished with simplicity. The bulkheads, except for one, held photographs of exotic, forbidding places. It appeared to Histor-Us there was a photo showing every landfall the No'mo had made during her years of service. Four chairs, bolted to the deck, were around a wooden topped table. It was the sort of table one expected to see covered with maps and graphs. On the far end of the table sat an open case containing black spheres as large as oranges.

A lean Orang of mid-height with a short sleeve shirt and captain's cap, slipped a piece of fruit in his mouth as he stepped aside leaving the floor exclusively to Sey-Us.

He would have been quite natural in a group of scientists, but he held an aura of iron will and bright eyes that showed a zest for living. Those eyes locked on Histor-Us in an intimidating stare. An impatient, demanding voice spoke withoiut any social amenities. It carried strangth, but to Histor-Us it was rude and demanding.

"It's about time you showed up, Histor-Us. I was just about to call you," Sey-Us said, as though he were addressing a first year student.

"If I had known I would have waited." Histor-Us eyed his

challenger uneasily. All the way down here for nothing, Histor-Us

thought. Might as well get this unpleasantness over with. Sey-Us caught him off balance by becoming the soul of social grace.

"This is the skipper, Captain Mai-Us," Sey-Us said, in a cordial tone. The captain held out a rough, furry hand. When he released Histor-Us' hand he moved the case of spheres to the far side of the table and sat down. Histor-Us turned his attention stiffly back to Sey-Us.

"You've met Risc-Um," Sey-Us said, and Histor-Us nodded to Risc-Um.

"Histor-Us, you just met a duo you would never come across in Simalia. Both were with me on my previous expeditions, and I'll say bluntly, if they weren't going on this one I would think twice before embarking on this voyage. I wouldn't have been successful on my expeditions if it hadn't been for these two. Where are my aides?" A silence was torn between one that chokes one when august praise has been bestowed and the expected answer to Sey-Us' abrupt inquiry.

Sey-Us leaned against the bulkhead and kept a critical look on the Institute's agent. Histor-Us stood defiantly for a moment before Sey-Us' stare got the better of him.

"What's going on with you, Histor-Us?" Sey-Us asked. "I was informed by Dr. Cari-Us that you would provide me with competent, healthy aides. So where are my aides?"

"I haven't found anyone stupid enough to volunteer," Histor-Us retorted, testily.

"Volunteers?" Sey-Us said, pushing away from the bulkhead. "Flaming hell! Talk sense will you." Risc-Um and Mai-Us were aware this daunting display was one of Sey-Us' tactics of intimidation. They knew he was angry at loosing his aides, and his anger was growing by a hedging lacky.

"See here, Histor-Us, let's understand one another and be reasonable. The Planetary Institute has funded this expedition. I'm then told my very able aides must return to the University. A more capable pair couldn't be found. I was also informed that you would replace my aides. That must be clear to the humblest of idiots. So what's this volunteer business?" Sey-Us paused and Histor-Us kept his eyes on him and remained silent.

"Tell me why you haven't assigned me aides?" Histor-Us felt a rush of defiance and wasn't about to let Sey-Us run over him.

"Everyone knows of your reputation for recklessness, Sey-Us. On
top of that, how do you hope to inspire confidence about this voyage
when you're being so damn secretive?"

"That's surely true," Mai-Us said, cutting another piece of fruit.

"The captain and mate don't even know where this ship is bound for," Risc-Um agreed, slowly rubbing his jaw.

This reinforced Histor-Us and he pumped up his rightoius attitude.

"There you are, Sey-Us, and from your own people." Histor-Us spread his hands palms up.

"How can I assign you aides without some idea of what they might expect? It seems to me you're asking for blind trust. I can't – no, I won't, become involved in such a mysterious venture." The anger could almost have been a blast from his eyes to Histor-Us.

"Flaming hell! What does your pea brain imagine my aides are to expect?" Histor-Us thought this was an opportunity. He lifted a hand and pushed a finger down for each point he made.

"First, you expect them to go off not knowing where or for how long. Second, you won't hint at why this ship has a crew twice its normal size. Third, how can you expect one to accept such bizarre circumstances?" Histor-Us was becoming more confident as he spoke. He resented Sey-Us' intransigent attatude.

"You don't understand, Histor-Us," Sey-Us said, crashing his hand on the table. "I'm setting out to make the greatest discovery of my career and I must have aides. They must be aboard without anymore delay." Histor-Us folded his arms and stiffened his posture.

"Why do you need aides? You seem more than capable. Why are you insisting on risking the lives of others?" Sey-Us frowned and stepped to within inches of Histor-Us.

"Do you think I want aides that will serve no purpose? No! I intend to sweat blood to make the most astonishing discovery of all time." He turned away from Histor-Us and slammed a fist into his palm.

"My goal is to bring back a living legend. I can't do that if my time is taken up with routine tasks that can be handled by aides. You're not a working field scientist, Histor-Us.

Therefore you have no comprehension of the procedures that must be followed."

The only words that made an impression on Histor-Us was living legend. It reminded him of what the old sailor had said. He saw Sey-Us was fuming, and he was an agent of the Institute that cared about his career. He resolved not to get involved in Sey-Us' scheme. Histor-Us felt he could handle any repercussions that might come from Dr. Cari-Us and was going to play it safe.

"I don't feel there's anyway I can be of service, Dr. Sey-Us," Histor-Us said, curtly. "Of course, this places me in an awkward position, but I have to do what I consider is best for all concerned." Sey-Us was steaming.

"I didn't put your lazy carcass in any position," Sey-Us said, trying hard to control his temper. "It was Cari-Us who put you in the position of assigning me aides for this expedition. By the Institue's rules, you're required to comply, Histor-Us." His outburst tended to make Histor-Us more stubborn.

"It's imperative we sail before dawn. It will be impossible to delay any longer."

"Why must you sail before dawn?" Histor-Us asked, suspicious. Sey-Us glanced at Mai-Us and Risc-Um then looked back to Histor-Us.

"I'll tell you," Sey-Us said, subtly trying to shift tactics. "We're carrying firearms and explosives. The Port Authority has gotten wind of it and will be down on our necks in the morning. That will mean a long legal contest that Cari-Us will frown on." He paused keeping his most intimidating glare on Histor-Us.

"It will be dangerous where we're going. It won't be as safe as sitting behind a desk, and I don't have time for your stalling tactics."

"Stalling tactics?" Histor-Us said, indignantly. "I feel you should clarify that." Sey-Us switched tactics again. Ignoring Histor-Us' demand, he went to the case on the table and picked up one of the black spheres. He eyed it lying in his hand with a proud look. Histor-Us was puzzled and at a loss to explain the change in Sey-Us.

"Far be it from me, Histor-Us, to tell you anyone would meet with no danger on this expedition. There will be danger. A little now and then, maybe even from the sea," he said, in a concillatory tone. "But you have my word that so long as these are handy no harm will come to any member of this expedition." He hefted the sphere.

"These negate any danger we might encounter, Histor-Us, except for the sea."

"And just what is that silly black sphere you boast to be your great protector?"

"A vapor bomb," Sey-Us said, tossing it into the air and catching it. "My own design." He looked at Histor-Us with a slight grin.

"I should say my improvement on the standard model. One of these silly spheres is enough to knock out a number of elephants(?)."

"Madness!" Histor-Us exclaimed, his nervousness apparent. "The
more I hear about this expedition, Sey-Us, the less I care for it. I must
say in all honesty, I'm glad to have the common sense not to
accommodate your request for aides." As soon as Histor-Us shut his mouth, Sey-Us tossed the sphere to him.
Frantically, Histor-Us managed just barely to grasp it. Sey-Us had really shaken him with the unexpected demonstration.

Risc-Um moved quickly beside him and relieved him of the sphere after he almost dropped it. Risc-Um's grin was most telling of his opinion of Histor-Us. Sey-Us was wagging a finger in his face.

"Histor-Us, you're being as stiff-necked as the Port Authority," Sey-Us said, in his most acid tone. "There's no more harm in one of those bombs as there is in a bunch of bananas(?) as long as they're handled by professionals who understand them." Histor-Us nervously rubbed his hands on his legs.

"I wouldn't let anyone use them who hadn't been properly trained," Sey-Us continued. "The brutal fact is the rainy season is likely to cause more trouble than anything we might run into. That's the vital factor in our sailing tomorrow." Sey-Us had done his best to convince Histor-Us that everything he said was above board.

"I trust the skipper and Risc-Um to sail the ship through storms, but field work requires dry, sunny weather. Of course, I don't expect an ace desk rider like yourself to understand that." Sey-Us stepped over and gave Risc-Um a comradely pat on the shoulder.

"The coming seaon in the Southern Hemisphere will bring heavy rain that in turn will produce a costly delay and show nothing for the labor. Nothing, Histor-Us!" Sey-Us paused again still hoping to convince him.

"You're not a scientist, but try to understand my position. I'm sanctioned by the Institute to undertake this expedition. When I return, Dr. Cari-Us will want to see what the Institute's expenditure has produced in real scientific advancement." Histor-Us was confused by the rational argument Sey-Us was now using, but it also tended to make his resolve stronger. He now had confidence in himself as he realized how desperate Sey-Us was. He had no intension of falling for the false sincerity.

Sey-Us had done a lot of talking but Histor-Us still knew nothing of their destination except for the remark about the Southern Hemisphere, nor the duration of their stay.

"Sey-Us you make me feel like a potential killer. I cannot, will not
sanction any such assignment." He went to the hatch, stopped, and
turned back to Sey-Us with a steady gaze.

"I've suffered enough abuse from you, Sey-Us. You will get no
aides through me, now or ever."

"What!"

"I'll not be responsible for getting someone killed in one of your wild adventures." A loud, annoyed snort came from Sey-Us.

"Go back to your desk. I don't need an Institute lacky like you to find me a competent field aide. I'll find one on my own." Being stocky, Sey-Us pushed past Histor-Us and yanked his jacket from the wall hook with agility. He was mad enough to have punched Histor-Us but refrained from the pleasure because time was short. He knew there wasn't time to contact Cari-Us, and Sey-Us wasn't calm enough to think of anything so sensible.

He stopped at the hatch and turned a killing glare on Histor-Us.

"If you think I'm going to be deterred because an Institute messenger doesn't have the gumption to do his job you better think again. That's assuming thoughts run through a little mind like yours." He jerked the hatch open.

"I'm going to make the greatest discovery of all time," Sey-Us said, loudly. "Something that's never been seen by civilized Simians.

They'll have to rewrite anthropology when I return. I'll show you, Histor-Us, and the rest of the fat, lazy desk riders what it means to be a scientist, and what can be accomplished in the field." He stepped through the hatch slamming it behind him.

Histor-Us looked indignant as he regarded Mai-Us and Risc-Um.

"Lazy! Lacky! Desk rider! Indeed his manners leave a lot to be desired." Mai-Us went to the hatch, opened it, and shouted into the darkness.

"Where are you going, Sey-Us?" Sey-Us' determined voice floated back as his footsteps sounded along the deck.

"To find an aide. I'll bring one back even if I have to resort to abduction." Histor-Us fumbled with the buttons on his jacket darting embarrassed glances at Mai-Us and Risc-Um. He had never been so humiliated. Stiff-necked! It was an absurd allegation, he felt. Secretly, he was elated to be rid of Sey-Us without becoming involved in this scheme. Yes, sir, Histor-Us thought. Crazy was the right word after all and it really applied to Sey-Us.

Risc-Um burst out in hearty laghter he couldn't contain any longer. It had been the most humerous confrontation it had been his pleasure to witness. He looked at Mai-Us.

"I'll bet he's back onboard with an aide before it's time to sail, Skipper." Mai-Us grinned and shook his head.

"I'll not take that bet. I know him too well," Mai-Us said, and slipped a piece of fruit into his mouth. Risc-Um looked to Histor-Us and shook his head.

"You don't know Sey-Us, Doctor. He wouldn't hesitate to order me to tie someone up and bring them aboard if he thought it would make for a successful expedition. I'll see you to your car."

THE NEW AIDE

Sey-Us left the No'mo in a forlorn hope of finding an aide. Anger still boiled in him as he passed through patchy fog, left the waterfront, and headed into Icense. Walking sullenly, he made straight for the University Campus. As he walked among the students watching and listening, he swore under his breath at what he considered the stupidity of that prize ass Histor-Us.

Ocassionally he caught part of an especially promising conversation only to hear it lapse into the mundane. Sey-Us concentrated his search around the Anthropology Hall and found that the night students were quite common when it came to their chosen field of study. His ears would pick up conversation, concentrate, and drop it as being too general in content.

He hoped to hear a student giving a brilliant dissertation to his classmates on the subject dear to Sey-Us' heart. That would be his new aide. With eyes narrowed and hearing acutely attuned he stubbornly continued with his search. Again and again he caught fragments of conversation, listened, then sadly discard what he had heard. He moved among the small gatherings of students but nowhere did Sey-Us discover the speaker that would have stood out, as I am the one you seek. Eventually, his unflagging will began to crumble against seemingly inevitable failure.

After an hour, and a growing headache brought on by desperation, did he turn back to the waterfront in bitter disappointment. Tramping along, he left the campus and prowled about the outlying areas. It was just too hard for him to give up and return to the ship. It wasn't in him to give up. The last thing Sey-Us wanted to admit, especially to himself, was that Histor-Us had won. He had never before in his life felt so utterly helpless. He was reluctant to face renewed failure among the students and didn't loiter.

He went to a fruit stand, bought an apple, and stood looking around. In the ensuing weeks, he would pat himself on the back for the luck that had caused him to double back to the fruit stand. It was small, hardly larger than a booth, but large enough to accommodate the Chimp proprietor and his stock. The place was so small the apples were on a rack at the front. The Chimp kept a wary eye on Sey-Us. Sey-Us had a better view of the apples than the Chimp and saw what happened. Although the event happened quickly, Sey-Us was certain of what he saw.

A young female Orang came slowly from the shadows to the fruit stand, reached out a slim hand and hungrily began to enclose it about one the red apples. With a brief glance at Sey-Us, he knew what her intension was. The Chimp was sharpeyed too and came crashing through the stand roaring mad.

"Finally I've caught one of you thieves," the Chimp said, loudly. "You've been stealing my fruit and getting away with it for too long.
I'm calling a deputy." He seized her hand quite viciously, taking her
by surprise at his sudden assault. At first she seemed too stunned to move , but as she became aware of her situation, she began to react feebly.

"No! Please let me go. I didn't steal anything. I wanted to, but didn't," she begged, and tried weakly to pull her arm from his grip. The Chimp glared at her.

"The only reason you didn't steal anything was because I caught you. Enough is enough! And I've had more than enough." His voice was hard, tense.

"She's telling the truth," Sey-Us said. "She was taking her hand off the apple when you came after her. She wasn't going to steal your fruit."

"I wasn't," she implored, hurriedly, in a frightened tone. "Truly I wasn't." Sey-Us took a good look at her face and a sudden flicker of memory came to mind. She seemed vaguely familiar. If his memory was correct, he had just encountered an incredible favor from fate. He couldn't be certain only from memory. She was silently appealing for Sey-Us to help her out of this predicament. The Chimp still held her wrist in a vise-like grip when Sey-Us stepped to him.

"Take this five note and forget it," Sey-Us said, with authority. It was the monetary note that reversed the Chimp's point of view. He took the note, let go of her wrist, and went back into the stand spilling thanks all the way.

Unexpectedly released, she would have collapsed had not Sey-Us quickly flung his arm arout her shoulders. Her head fell against him, eyes closed. The amber light from above fell on her face and Sey-Us got a close look. He studied her face for a moment, his eyes widened, and he felt like yelling. His memory had made a correct identification. Once again, fate had smiled on him, but he needed to talk with her. He emitted a soft triumphant laugh as he raised his hand to signal.

"Taxi," he called. One pulled to the curb, Sey-Us opened the door, set the female on the seat and climbed in.

In a white tiled dinning room, Sey-Us felt she was a special gift from a generous destiny. In the chair opposite him, the now familiar female sat behind a stack of tan empty dishes. She hadn't spoken while she ate, and he had respected her silence. Leaning forward, Sey-Us looked thankful. Once he had become certain of who she was he had silently rejoiced at his incredible luck.

Large brown eyes regarded him and a grateful smile appeared. She finished the grape juice, sat the glass down and regarded him steadily.

So far she had shown no sign of recognizing him.

"Feeling better?" Sey-Us asked.

"Yes, thank you. I'm Ihand-A again. You've been very kind to me and I feel I know you. Anyway, I appreciate what you've done." Her voice expressed contentment.

"Don't be so quick to take my generosity for granted," Sey-Us said, in his usual blunt manner. "I didn't spend money on you just out of kindness." He ignored her remark about knowing him. The contentedness quickly faded from Ihand-A. She trembled as she kept her eyes on him trying to define the meaning of his words.

"You don't recognize me. Well it has been over a year since I last saw you. I often wondered what happened when you abruptly failed to show up for my classes." Her eyes narrowed.

"You do look familiar. Yet I can't place you." Sey-Us leaned back and regarded her for a moment.

"I'm curious as to how you ended up in such conditions," he said, genuine concern in his tone. He was curious about her sudden drop in the social strata.

"I could say it was bad luck," she begun, feeling she owed him for his kindness. "Maybe I should have been smarter, but that would have side stepped the problem. To put it clearly, I was kicked out of the University and blacklisted because I wouldn't play sweet little sleep in with an influencial professor." Sey-Us was shocked and at a loss for words. He felt a deep sense of shame that a fellow academic, and instructor, could be so vile. At that moment, he wished he had stayed aboard the No'mo. The more he thought the more he knew he need not feel shame but outrage, and he got angrier the longer he thought about it.

"So that's what happened," Sey-Us said. "That explains your reaction to what I said. I missed you in my class as you were a top student. I'm Dr. Sey-Us."

"Oh." It took her a few minutes to recall fourteen months past because of all that occurred in the interval. She slowly nodded.

"Yes, Dr. Sey-Us. I'm sorry for what I said about a fellow professor. I hope you won't say anything to anyone about it. I've had enough trouble in the last year to last a lifetime." He noted her fearful expression. She felt she had said the wrong thing to the wrong person and the idea of what that might entail frightened her. Sey-Us waved his hand.

"No need to worry, Ihand-A I detest anyone who takes personal

advantage of their position," Sey-Us said, in an angry tone. But he still had to talk to her about the expedition, time was growing short.

"Are you still interested in anthropology? If so, would you be willing to leave in the morning on an expedition as my aide?" Sey-Us rattled it off quickly, hoping she would accept. She stared in surprise.

"Of course I'm interested in anthropolgy, enough so that I would like to get my doctorate in the field." He saw she was excited and brightening to the prospect.

"Working for you as an aide would prove challenging and an honor." Relief filled Sey-Us as he watched her eyes brighten.

"Good. Can you leave in the morning?" She nodded.

"Certainly. I have no family to speak of, and all of my used to be friends shun me. I certainly won't be missed by anyone." Sey-Us silently gloated at the thought that idiot Histor-Us had been overcome. He had accomplished what he said he would, found an aide.

Under the circumstances, a better one couldn't have been found. He recalled that Ihand-A had been an exceptionally bright student with a talent for fieldwork.

He pushed the chair from the table and stood. Ihand-A hesitated for a moment then stood. Their gaze met and she wanted to hear him say it, and got a puzzled expression.

"What's wrong?" he asked, concerned that she might be considering changing her mind. It was clear he wasn't reading her, so she chose to speak bluntly. Talking about such a personal thing didn't come easy, but she had to be truthful.

"Dr. Sey-Us, I've had a difficult time because I wouldn't grant a
professor special favors." Now he knew her concern.

"Let me put your mind at ease, Ihand-A Our relationship will be as professionals of science. We'll be working together as field researchers." He grinned and patted her arm.

"Besides, I'm too old for what's worrying you. I want you, no I need you, on my expedition because my aides were recalled to Samalia, and the bungling clod who was supposed to assign me new aides refused because I wouldn't divulge my destination." He spoke so she could think over what he said. She smiled as he saw in her eyes an alert, intelligent mind waiting and wanting to work.

"I've been planning this expedition for two years. I'll have no inclination for the sort of sordid position my unknown colleague tried to force you into. Clear?"

"Yes, Dr. Sey-Us, and I believe you." He knew she now trusted
him, but he was still curious.

"His name wouldn't have been Histor-Us by any chance?" he asked, quickly. She gave him a puzzled look.

"Who?" He quickly waved a hand.

"Never mind. He isn't intelligent enough to think of something like that. Sorry I asked."

"I'm out of practice on field procedures, Doctor. You'll have to coach me for awhile." Her tone was confident.

"As for field procedure, it will have to be made up since this expedition will have unusual aspects. Both of us will learn as we discover conditions. Now we must get you suitable attire for the tropics. Shall we go?" She nodded.

"Lead on." He smiled and patted her arm.

"After we board the No'mo, you'll have a few days to rest, then I'll show you how I want field reports done. I don't think you'll have any problem picking up right where you left off, Ihand-A." She got a confused look.

"This is all happening so fast it seems like a dream."

"My dear, the dream doesn't start until early tomorrow morning when we depart on a long sea voyage. When we return, we shall have our names put in the history books and make them rewrite the standard texts on anthropology." Sey-Us was bubbling with the spirit of adventure gleaming brightly on his horizon. He was ready to confront anything Scumm Island might put in front of him. He would, naturally, take the unknown in his stride and conquer it. He felt he was doing it for science, but the financial reward also had to be considered, in this case in particular. He felt unbeatable and knew he could win regardless of the odds, and tonight had proven it.

"Is there anything in particular I should know, Dr. Sey-Us?" She was becoming imbued with the excitement coming from him. He tucked a finger under her chin.

"Keep your courage and trust me. Everything will turn out all right." He bowed his arm and waited for her. He looked at her with pride. He had always been lucky, he reminded himself, despite idiots like Histor-Us.

His grateful gaze didn't falter as she slipped her arm through his and they walked into the clear warm night of Icense.

DEPARTURE

Ihand-A slowly opened her eyes from the light sleep as she lay in a soft berth. For a moment, she couldn't recall where she was or how she came to be here. She only knew that this was a morning in a very long time that she awoke without a troubled mind. The odor of fresh bedding kept her wrapped in its softness awhile longer. Wondering what had given her such peace of mind, she remembered her incredible encounter with Dr. Sey-Us.

She sat up and saw the bowl of apples, and lightly laughed. Sey-Us had bought them adding to the bulk of clothing that had crowded them into a corner of the taxi seat. It had been after midnight when they boarded the No'mo. Sey-Us had disappeared for a few minutes and returned with a shallow bowl. It looked silly then and looked doubly silly now.

"This bowl will have to do." She recalled him saying with a grin. Holding the bowl and apples and balancing packages with one arm, she had followed him. Sey-Us was also loaded down with packages as he led the way along the dim, narrow passageway to a white wooden door.

"This is your cabin," he had said, opening the door and turning on the light. He put the packages on the floor and turned to her.

"If it makes you feel more comfortable, you can lock the door. I want you to get a good night's sleep. Sleep as long as you like. I prefer my aide to be bright and alert. I'll see you in the morning." He had stepped out the door and pulled it shut behind him.

Ihand-A glanced at the clock on the bulkhead. It was the only thing on any of them except for the porthole above the clock. It was just shy of ten. She had been dozing for nine hours. Except for her last doze, she had slept soundly and felt quite rested and eager to start her new job.

She couldn't suppress her excitement and laughed again. She felt happy and determined not to let anything spoil such a wonderful feeling. It was time to go on deck and look around.

She recalled Sey-Us telling her that Captain Mai-Us was stern and gruff, but nice. But it was the first mate, Risc-Um, she wanted to meet. According to Sey-Us, he was young and tough, but a decent person. A most intriguing description for an inquisitive female. She dressed and tossed her old clothes in the trash container beside the door. She turned to the open porthole and inhaled the clean air of the ocean.

Sey-Us' promised departure had been made shortly before dawn. Icense had already vanished below the horizon and only the snow capped mountain peaks were still visible. Around the ship stretched endless, empty ocean calmly undelating in blue-gray water that spread to the horizon and merged with the sky. The breeze was from the south and warm.

Ihand-A turned back to the clothing parcels and felt the urge to get the cabin tidied up before going on deck. She was overflowing with an eagerness that enhanced her energy. She attacked the pile of packages that had been scattered across the floor where Sey-Us and she had put them. The vibrations of the No'mo's throbbing engines made her legs feel as if they were pulsing with the deck. She began putting the packages in the space under her berth. It took sometime, and a lot of rearranging, but finally they were neatly stowed.

Ihand-A had opened each before putting it away trying to decide what to wear on deck. The dress she wore was definitely not for being on deck. As a consequence of her surrender to pleasure, it was almost eleven before she stepped into the deserted passageway.

She felt ready for work in her tan jumpsuit. Whatever Sey-Us had told her, she was prepared to start today. She had never known such an intoxicating state of euphoria.

She found the deck almost as deserted as the passageway. Ihand-A didn't take long to conclude that crew and officers, having cleared details of departure, had resumed other duties. She saw a sailor in a sheltered corner sprawled in the sun. A vertiable ancient Chimp, his dark fur was tinged with gray, as he sat humming softly as he tied knots for lines of the rigging. Stealthily, she moved closer to him. Because he had such a friendly face, and she felt so happy, she dropped suddenly beside him.

"Could that knot help one to scale a cliff? Would you teach me to
tie those knots?" she asked, excited at being on the ship. He regarded her with no surprise apparent.

"Yes, young lady, to both questions." She then knew he had heard her first sly steps toward him. She was surprised as the tone of his voice told her that Sey-Us had let it be known she was aboard. She still felt welcomed on the ship.

"Let me intoduce myself," he said, in a strong eastern drawl. "I'm Pablae, deckhand first class."

"I'm Ihand-A, Dr. Sey-Us' aide."

"Sure as sunrise. The crew have been told about you. I'll show you how to tie this knot."

To Ihand-A, he seemed to be doing aimless but expert moves with the rope. His agile fingers quickly had the knot taking shape and held it up.

"This is a running bowline. All you need do is rise, arc, and glide down. It's simple, as knots go. Here, Miss, give it a try." She took the rope, but her eyes drifted over the blue-gray expanse surronding her.

"Oh, Pablae, it feels wonderful here," she said, in a voice brimming with enthusiasm.

She still had trouble accepting the contrast from only a day ago. So much had changed so quickly she still felt locked in a dream. Pablae got a longing look.

"Me, I would rather be putting down a tall cold one in the Ocean Paradise," he said, honestly wishing he was there. "But I guess it's everyone to their own poison, I always say."

"I guess it isn't nice or safe out here when the sea turns rough, is it? Does it get very frightening during a storm? Here on the ship, I mean." Ihand-A wanted to pick up as much information as she could. Pablae tilted his head.

"It certainly is nice to have the sea like glass and the sun riding high in a clear sky," he admitted, rising hastily as a whistle blew shrilly.

There was a second and a third blast as it neared where she sat. Warmed to complacency by the sun and the throb of the engines, she kept to her sheltered corner as Pablae moved quickly toward the midship hold. She was surprised as to his agility for one his age.

On the last note from the whistle, a few more sailors rushed forward into view. Ihand-A's eyes moved to the companionway by which she had came on deck and saw the whistle and its master. He was young and intent on his work and failed to notice his silent audience. At the sight of him, Ihand-A's interest in the situation grew. His trim well muscled body, his strong blond face and air of being master and knowing it, challenged her directly in a fashion that she found not at all unpleasant. She decided this was First Mate Risc-Um.

He took a position that presented his back to her as she stood and moved forward for a better view, as her interest was aroused. He wore an officer's cap and a green silk shirt she felt could not easily be afforded on a sailor's pay.

The sailors gathered in front of him and he proceeded to put them to work. They were opening a hold to lower a crate from the deck into it.

What, to Ihand-A, seemed to be a tangled mass of ropes was to be the means of lifting and lowering it, if it could be disentangled. She moved away from the bulkhead in order to observe the midship deck. Risc-Um continued giving orders in a loud, rapid-fire voice. A sailor let go of the rope he had been holding, letting it dangle and making no effort to retrieve it.

"You! Get hold of that rope or I'll feed you to the fish," Risc-Um roared. The sailor stared dumbly at the rope until Risc-Um bellowed causing him to grasp the rope.

"Not that one. The one to your starboard and make sure you hold it fast." The sailors seemed to be getting the tangle straightened out.

"You there, pick up that line and haul it to port. To your port. All of you move it to the hatch." When he motioned to port, he swung his arm in that direction. With a full, furious sweep, his hand struck bitingly across Ihand-A's cheek.

"What?" Risc-Um said, turning. She had reeled back toward the sun-warmed nook and almost fell. Her face stung hotly and her eyes clouded. Risc-Um turned to see what he had hit and checked himself when he saw her. He quickly knew he liked what his eyes locked onto.

"What are you doing up here? Sey-Us said you were in your cabin. You're not supposed to be sneaking around on deck," he said, sternly, as if repremanding her like one of the sailors.

"I was not sneaking around," Ihand-A replied, angrily, rubbing her cheek. "I came up for fresh air and to watch. I'm no concern of yours."

Her voice slipped from anger to indignation, aware that what had happened had been her fault for not letting him know of her presence. It was difficult for her not to be intimidated by his eyes.

"I apologize. I hope my hand didn't land too hard," Risc-Um said, softening under the changing tone of her voice.

"There's no need to apologize. It was my fault. You didn't know I
was here and I got in your way. It really doesn't hurt that much." Her voice rose so fast they began to laugh and quickly felt relaxed.

"So you're the field aide Sey-Us found at the last minute." He was feeling ill at ease looking at her and couldn't understand why.

"A most grateful and excited aide," she said, feeling exultation returning. "This is all new to me as it's the first time I've ever been on a ship. I'm so excited I couldn't sleep." Risc-Um nodded.

"I've never been on a ship with a single female," Risc-Um said. "Sey-Us usually has a male or couples for his aides. This time he was pressed for time and…" He let his words trail off. With his change of attitude, Ihand-A felt he was a gruff sailor. But she was uncertain as to how to take his change toward her.

"Just what are you trying to say? That you don't approve of a
single female aide, or you don't think much of a female on a ship?"
Risc-Um had to quickly adjust to her.

"I don't want any misunderstanding about my opinion. I know Sey-Us had no choice in the matter. But a female on an expedition like this could be a dangerous distraction." He quickly held up a hand before she could respond.

"I don't have anything against you. It's just my opinion." She stiffened her posture and regarded him indignantly.

"I shall do my best not to be a distraction, especially to you, Mr. Risc-Um." The words came stiffly as she didn't care having her elation spoiled by a rude, overbearing sea going chauvinist.

"You've already gotten in the way," he pointed out, bluntly. It was bluff as he tried to cover his odd feelings with rudness.

"You better stay in your cabin. You'll be out of the crew's way and won't be stumbling around underfoot." Ihand-A stared at him.

"You have a lot to learn about females, Mr. Risc-Um. I'll make it easy by not speaking to you." She was angered at what he suggested. He looked into her eyes and quickly averted his to hide his confusion. He was aware of his shyness and tried his best to hide it. Sensing this, Ihand-A felt a new confidence and a sudden soft feeling for the hard Mr. Risc-Um. The last thing she had expected of someone with his temperament was shyness.

"I didn't mean the whole voyage," he relented, slowly. "You can come on deck once in a while." He was unsuccessful in suppressing a silly, unwanted grin.

"Does your cheek still smart? That was a pretty hard hit." He spoke in a mild tone.

"Don't worry," Ihand-A replied. "I can take it. Life lately has been one slap in the face after another." Risc-Um looked at her and the strange feeling surged in him.

"If it's been that rough for you, we're just going to have to make things a little easier for you," he said, softly.

Once more their eyes met and Ihand-A became flustered when she saw Sey-Us standing regarding them. He had quickly assessed the situation and came over to them. He had a frown but a proud expression.

"I told you to get a long sleep," Sey-Us said, sternly, keeping his eyes on her.

"I slept as long as I could, Dr. Sey-Us. I felt it would be a waste of time to lounge in the cabin," she said, with a hesitant smile. Sey-Us nodded and turned to Risc-Um. He glanced back at Ihand-A

"I see you've become acquainted with Risc-Um. What do you think of the No'mo's first mate?" She gave Risc-Um a cursory look.

"He's all right, I guess. But I find he's somewhat out of step with the times. Other than that, he's friendly enough." Sey-Us turned his gaze to Risc-Um and mumbled something. Risc-Um glanced quickly from Sey-Us to Ihand-A wondering what had passed silently between them, and suspected it to be one of Sey-Us' pranks.

"I never claimed to be easy to get along with," Risc-Um said, defensively. "It comes with the job." As Sey-Us burst out laughing, Risc-Um gave Ihand-A a perplexed look.

"I must say the future looks most interesting," Sey-Us said.

"What are you talking about?" Risc-Um asked, confused. He kept glancing at Ihand-A unable to determine if she was in on Sey-Us' prank. She returned a puzzled look. Was there anything going on? Risc-Um wondered.

"You'll learn in your own good time, Risc-Um," Sey-Us said, and turned his attention to Ihand-A He waved toward her cabin.

"Since you're awake and eager we may as well start," Sey-Us said. "Go to your cabin and bring up the field kit. Our destination is the Forgotten Zone. That's all you need know for now. Run along." She started for her cabin.

"That's all the skipper and I know," Risc-Um said. Sey-Us nodded.

"When it's time, I'll reveal everything. For now, I must keep our destination secret." It was Risc-Um's statement that stopped Ihand-A in midstep. Sey-Us turned and saw her.

"I'll tell you at the same time, Ihand-A," Sey-Us said. "I want to test you and see how much you recall of field procedures. Think you remember enough to pass your first test?" Ihand-A nodded.

"I believe so," she replied, turned, and went toward her cabin. She glanced back at Risc-Um, almost getting over her anger.

When Ihand-A turned into the passageway, Risc-Um faced his boss with a scowl.

"You should have given her some idea of what she was getting into, Sey-Us. Your not confiding in the skipper and me leads me to believe you've really got a bug under the cover this time."

"Tell her?" Sey-Us asked, with a look of surprise. "And have you trying to charm it out of her? Oh, no, Risc-Um. I'll tell her when I tell you and the skipper." Sey-Us looked toward the passageway with swelling pride.

"How do you like the spirit of my aide?" Risc-Um rubbed his
cheek.

"She has an independent mind and should make an able aide – if you can control her temper." Sey-Us patted Risc-Um's shoulder.

"That I agree with. She used to be a student of mine a year or so past. A very bright student, I might add. Unfortunately she had a falling out with bad company."

"She's certainly not the sort of aide you usually have."

"No, but I was lucky to find her. I know she's going to prove more efficient than anyone that moron Histor-Us could have assigned."

"I'm wondering if any female should be along. After all, this venture might prove more dangerous than you think. And before you say anything, Sey-Us, yes I'm concerned about her." Sey-Us regarded him slightly disturbed since this was the first time he had known Risc-Um to display such emotion.

"Flaming hell! You better keep your mind on your duty, Risc-Um. You're going to be in deep water quickly. Come along and help me with the chart so you can have a clearer idea of the area we're heading for. Sey-Us dropped the hint he knew would spark Risc-Um's curiosity and take his mind off Ihand-A

THE VOYAGE

Risc-Um ordered the crew to complete stowing the crate and followed Sey-Us to the bridge. The sailors had been pleasantly interrupted by the show between the first mate and Ihand-A. It seemed to them this might prove to be an unforgettable voyage.

Ihand-A came on the bridge carrying a large suede case by a shoulder strap. She realized Sey-Us had put it in her cabin after she had gone out. It had been no accident that he had been coming from that direction. The field suit she now wore made her attractive appearance seem more like a person of business, and the sailors took more notice than before.

"Now she looks like an anthropologist," Risc-Um remarked, dourly, unable to take his eyes from her. Sey-Us delighted at the impulsive tribute, but ignored Risc-Um's tone.

"She surely does," Sey-Us said, proudly. Risc-Um was mesmerized by her and Sey-Us took note of it.

"I don't think she looks like your average anthropologist, do you, Risc-Um?" Sey-Us asked, in his usual blunt manner. Risc-Um glanced at him.

"Not by any means," Risc-Um agreed. Sey-Us' chest expanded at his words. But he was concerned about Risc-Um's sudden emotional attachment to Ihand-A and this brought on an almost paternal pride in him.

Ihand-A put the kit on the table and opened it.

"I checked it, Dr. Sey-Us, and the kit is complete." As she spoke, she kept glancing at Risc-Um then turned her attention to Sey-Us.

"Is something wrong, Doctor?" she asked, puzzled.

"No, Ihand-A I'm glad you could see the kit was complete. I told you it wouldn't be difficult for you to remember." She smiled.

"It was rather easy."

"You haven't forgotten a thing I taught you," Sey-Us said, proudly. Ihand-A was pleased but wondered at the odd glances between Risc-Um and Sey-Us.

"Keep the kit in your cabin. Later, I'll give you copies of reports so you'll know how to make them out." She moved in obedience to her benefactor's gesture of dismissal.

Pablae and half a dozen sailors stood outside the bridge watching intently, their eyes riveted on Ihand-A Having a female onboard was a novelty to most of them. Three years past, Odeer-A and Gonail-Um had been Sey-Us' aides, but they had been engaged. It wasn't the same as having a female aboard that could back Risc-Um down. That's what amazed them. Females, it was devoutly believed by sailors, sailed only on liners, not the working ships.

Mai-Us appeared glaring at the gawking sailors and faced them.

"Who is manning the ship?" Mai-Us demanded, sternly. The
sailors quietly and quickly moved back to their duty. Mai-Us went back on the bridge, cut a piece of fruit, and regarded Ihand-A

"No wonder the crew is curious," Mai-Us said, smiling, and popped the piece of fruit in his mouth.

They spread the map on the table and looked over what was known about the Forgotten Zone. Glancing from Mai-Us, to Risc-Um, to Ihand-A, Sey-Us stepped to the table and began moving his finger on the map south.

"We'll maintain our present course for five days," Sey-Us said. "Then after we turn southwest into the Oi Sea, I'll reveal our destination."

"Why not now?" Risc-Um asked. Sey-Us gave him an annoyed look.

"Because I don't want the crew talking a lot of superstitious
drivel," Sey-Us replied. Risc-Um was irritated at Sey-Us' play on words.

"You told me we would find out where we were going," Risc-Um said. Sey-Us shook his head.

"I said you would get an idea of where we're going," Sey-Us said. He walked from the bridge before anyone could say anything more.

Mai-Us later returned to the bridge chewing on a slice of fruit. He noted Risc-Um's distraction and thought he knew the reason.

"You know how stubborn he can be when he's determined to have his way," Mai-Us said. Risc-Um turned to him.

"He's getting to me, Skipper. The secrecy isn't like Sey-Us. He's never acted this way before." Mai-Us nodded feeling the mate's frustration.

"We've done pretty well with him so far," Mai-Us said. "I agree he seems rather eccentric this time, but remember his reference to superstitious drivel." Mai-Us suddenly felt that wasn't the only thing on Risc-Um's mind. He had never heard him complain before and his distraction didn't seem to match what he voiced. Risc-Um saw the look he was getting from Mai-Us and felt he need explain.

"With her onboard, it makes it different this time, Skipper." Mai-Us stopped chewing and looked at Risc-Um. He knew now what was really distracting him.

"Sey-Us' aide is his responsibility, Risc-Um. Not yours or mine." Risc-Um was in emotional turmoil and at a loss to exp0lain it.

The more he thought about it the more determined he became in trying to change Ihand-A's mind about accompanying Sey-Us until they knew if there was danger. But she would still be on the ship and he wouldn't be able to avoid her.

"I've got to know what he's taking her into, Skipper." Mai-Us read his tone easily enough. He stepped to Risc-Um and clasped his shoulder.

"This is kind of sudden, isn't it?" Risc-Um got a helpless look.

"Too sudden! She's got some attraction... something about her... I can't control it." Mai-us dropped his arm to his side and rubbed his jaw.

"Better get control of yourself, Risc-Um. If not, it could cause you heartache." Now that Mai-Us knew their course, he decided to open up the old girl.

"Take over, Risc-Um. Bring her to full ahead." Risc-Um stepped forward and rang up full ahead on the annunciator. The engine room responded, ringing back that the order had been received. The speaker on the console crackled into life.

"Chief here, sir."

"This is Risc-Um, Chief. Nurse all the speed you can out of the engines."

"Aye, Mr. Risc-Um." He turned back to Mai-Us who was slipping another slice of fruit into his mouth. He didn't let it show, but he was concerned at Risc-Um's strong attraction for Ihand-A.

"We have to trust Sey-Us just as we did on the previous voyages. Let him worry about his aide and save yourself the concern."

"But, Skipper –" Mai-Us shook his head emphatically.

"No, buts, Risc-Um. We'll come through this all right.

Sey-Us knows what he's doing or I don't think he would have brought her. Haven't you noticed the way he looks at her? She's the child he never had, and he's proud of her." He patted Risc-Um's shoulder and left the bridge. Risc-Um turned to the table where the chart lay, stepped to it, and marked in their course toward the spot Sey-Us had indicated. Angrily, he slashed a red X on the map. He considered what Mai-Us had said, and felt he was right. He knew how he felt too, even if it was for the wrong reason. Risc-Um had no idea what he could do, or even if he should do anything.

The No'mo's prow sliced through the warm, endless sea. Wave after ceaseless wave of froth rolled along her flanks and joined the boiling white wake astern. All waters were the same to the ship needing only the power of its engines to keep it plunging ahead. Those engines throbbed with a constancy like life itself. They had last carried the crew and Sey-Us to explore the ice covered Northern Continent and returned them safely.

The days, like the miles, passed placidly away. They slowly transited the Anka Coral Shoals and past the Verun Islands. They had made a stop at Panjay for fuel, then sailed west past the Smophes Isles, turned south at Pizzo and eventually passed Butra at the northern edge of the Forgotten Zone.

The No'mo pushed on at a steady twenty-two knots, her direction south. The weather was growing sultry and the heat so uncomfortable that the crew wore only such garments as courtesy to Ihand-A called for. Pablae sprawled in a small patch of shade, bared to the waist. He showed ribs that a spectator could count, covered with tightly drawn skin. They protruded from his brown graying fur like small arches.

From his waist hung a pair of frayed pants that stopped just above his boney knees. It was attire aptly suited to the prevailing conditions.

Yet it could have been hotter considering the No'mo was just north of the equator.

Risc-Um wore shorts and a muscle shirt and was cool. He was cool until he grew impatient at the failure of a certain person to make an appearance. Ihand-A came on deck in a white jumpsuit that was armless and stopped just above her sandaled feet and she had a soft brimmed hat to shade her face. She stopped where Pablae lay. His eyes were closed but she didn't think he was asleep.

"Good afternoon, Pablae," she said, softly. He looked up shading his eyes and got a smile.

"Glad to see you about, Ihand-A." Risc-Um joined them and looked at her.

"What kept you?" Risc-Um queried, impatiently. As usual, his well rehearsed monologue began falling apart as soon as she was close.

"I was about to get to you," she replied, flashing a smile.

"What have you been doing? I've gotten lonesome."

"Crashing textbooks and checking field reports. You couldn't have gotten that lonesome in six hours."

"I thought it had been a week," Risc-Um said, smiling. He changed to a more immediate subject.

"Any chance you came across a clue as to where we're going?" She shook her head.

"Wherever it is, Dr. Sey-Us isn't taking a chance of it being discovered by accident. He's being so cautious as to recheck the dates on each report before he has me examine it." Risc-Um thoughtfully rubbed his chin. What could he be up to? Risc-Um wondered.

"What sort of reports has he had you reading?"

"Standard field reports from previous expeditions. He wants me to study them so I can standardize them."

"I wouldn't have you doing anything so dull," Risc-Um said, with a garish smile. She patted his arm.

"That I know, Risc-Um," she said, dryly. "I'm lucky you aren't the expedition director. From the reports I've read, Sey-Us thinks very highly of you. Your name is associated with such words as resourceful, inventive, courageous, and intelligent." Risc-Um was surprised to learn that Sey-Us had mentioned him in his reports.

"If I were the boss, you wouldn't be here ready to take risks that could put you in danger," Risc-Um said, turning sullen at the thought.

"That's very rude, Risc-Um You don't know the circumstances that brought me here. How do you know what the risk might be? If I hadn't had the blind luck to cross paths with Dr. Sey-Us, I would have been risking my life. Now I have a useful role to fulfill." She spoke angrily. Risc-Um got a look of annoyance and frustration.

"That isn't what I'm talking about, Ihand-A, and you know it." He lapsed into sullen silence despite the longing tug of her liquid eyes. How he always managed to say the wrong thing was a mystery to him, and it happened almost everytime they spoke.

"I like having you here," Risc-Um said. "But what are you here for? In a pinch, Sey-Us could have trained one of the crew to do what he has you doing. What sort of crazy thing is he after this time? When we get to wherever we're going, what will you have to face?" She was giving him a very annoyed look.

"I'll handle any situation as it develops," she said, coldly. "I don't care why he's keeping the destination secret. But no matter where we go, or what he asks of me, I'll do it.

I wouldn't have this chance if it hadn't been for him. He has my loyalty and that's the way it stands." She arced her arms from the bow to the stern.

"Furthermore, I've had the happiest time of my life on this ship." She finished folding her arms.

"Are you really happy?" he asked, surprised. She nodded.

"I'm not in the habit of saying things I don't mean." She quickly turned to some flattery.

"Everyone's been so nice –" She was interrupted as Pablae got to his feet. They had forgotten he was there.

"Mr. Risc-Um, I don't think I should be hearing a personal conversation. If you don't mind I'll find another shaded spot." He walked off toward the stern with them looking after him and feeling embarrassed.

"Where were we before the interruption?" Risc-Um asked, wishing Pablae hadn't heard their little spat.

"I was saying how nice everyone's been. Pablae and you, Dr. Sey-Us and Captain Mai-Us. You have to admit the captain's a really sweet apple." Risc-Um erupted in laughter looking around hoping none of the crew had heard what she had said. He shook his head as he got control of his laughter.

"Have you any idea of the uproar it would cause if anyone but me heard you call him that?" She looked surprised.

"You mean he wouldn't consider it a compliment?" she asked,
innocently, knowing the answer but wanting to play coy with Risc-Um.

"No one on board but you could say that and avoid being tossed into a hold in chains. That includes Sey-Us, who by the way, never uses terms of endearment for anyone but himself."

50

They locked arms and slowly strolled along the railing idly gazing down on the sea. Suddenly it was filled with countless tiny leaping splinters that, on closer examination, revealed themselves to be small fish. They noted each was fitted with a dorsal fin and each could have easily fit in the palm of a hand. They were going along with the ship as Ihand-A recalled Pablae had called them sea shippers. Ihand-A and Risc-Um were content as they turned back along the deck.

DISCLOSURE

During the voyage, Ihand-A and Risc-Um grew close, although he was still reserved in her company. He now felt at ease with her and told her about his decision to go to sea rather than the University. It had been the one way he could escape the dullness of becoming a civil engineer. He spoke of his parents, who had eventually forgiven him, and bolstered themselves to the dangers of the adventures he had been through with Sey-Us. They believed every voyage was filled with peril, and moreso after he had teamed up with Sey-Us. He and his father still didn't see eye to eye, and whenever they were together there was friction his mother tried to control. There had been times when both father and son had gotten out of line with each other and a heated argument had ensued. Risc-Um admitted that before he met Sey-Us, the life of a ship's officer had been rather routine. But it was never like that on one of Sey-Us' expeditions.

Ihand-A told him of the untimely death of her parents and the unstealing of an apple that had reintroduced her to Sey-Us. Her father had wanted her to become a doctor but she had a yen for prehistory and had decided on anthropolgy. She spoke bitterly of a deceitful aunt, whom she had trusted, of squandering her inheritance, except for her collage fund and she couldn't touch it. She related the difficult time she had gone through after being expelled from the university, her dispairing quest for work, and the constant hunger. Speaking of this, her tone became caustic and resentful. Risc-Um sympathized with her and understood her loyalty to Sey-Us. It didn't alleviate the unease he felt for her safety as he knew Sey-Us was prone to taking risks.

"I was alone, Risc-Um. I felt very lucky when Dr. Sey-Us found me. No telling what might have happened to me by now if he hadn't." She shuddered at the thought.

"What a somber conversation." They turned their faces and saw Sey-Us standing with his arms folded regarding them. The relationship between them had bothered him until he saw them work out their differences.

"More tests, reports, or books?" Risc-Um asked, scowling. Ihand-A kept a trusting look on Sey-Us as he rocked on his feet. Since Ihand-A had come aboard, he had been surprised at what Risc-Um thought him capable of. But he's right, Sey-Us thought. Risc-Um's insight amazed him and he decided to add that as another of his strong points.

"Nothing to get excited about, Risc-Um," Sey-Us replied, genially. "When you can, Ihand-A, get your field kit ready. You know what we'll need to be within easy reach." She nodded.

"I'll go and secure it." She walked briskly toward the passageway. Sey-Us took an apple from his pocket, leaned against the rail, and took a bite. He took out another and offered it to Risc-Um who shook his head. Risc-Um folded his arms so they stood out as distinct lumps as he thought it time to press for answers.

"From what you said to Ihand-A, I take it we'll be reaching our destination soon." Sey-Us glanced at him with no change of expression.

"I want everything ready when the time comes. Preparedness
negates mistakes." He took another bite knowing what Risc-Um
wanted to know and he was about to divulge.

"When are you going to tell us where we're going?"

"Soon." His evasiveness annoyed Risc-Um.

"What happens when we get there?" Sey-Us turned a surprised look to him.

"I'm not a seer, Risc-Um, only a scientist." The frustration Risc-Um felt grew knowing Sey-Us had never been this deceptive.

"You always knew before, Sey-Us. You must have some idea. You always knew and proved it to be true." Sey-Us felt complimented.

"I've no idea what we'll discover this time. It's too intangible." Sey-Us tossed the core over the side and turned to Risc-Um. He was aware of the cause of Risc-Um's concern, and he felt responsible for Ihand-A too.

"You going soft on me, Risc-Um?" Risc-Um frowned.

"You know better than that."

"Then why the interest about possible discoveries? You never asked before."

"I'm not afraid for myself and you know it. But Ihand-A —"

"Oh, so that's what this is about," Sey-Us said, coolly. He knew the answer before Risc-Um had spoken her name but felt it better to get it in the open. He also decided to tease Risc-Um to make his point rather try talking sense to him.

"So you've gone overboard for her. Better put the relationship on hold, Risc-Um. We don't need a love affair to complicate our other problems." He regarded Risc-Um with a proud look. Risc-Um was surprised that Sey-Us thought there was a love relationship between Ihand-A and himself.

"I thought you would have learned by now that she does pretty well looking out for herself."

"Love?" Risc-Um asked, in a self-justifying tone. "I'm concerned for her safety, that's all.

If you had kept your aides, I wouldn't have thought twice about them." Sey-Us nodded.

"I see. Odeer-A was married, Ihand-A isn't. It never seems to fail, Risc-Um." He gave Sey-Us a puzzled look.

"What are you talking about, Sey-Us?" He was surprised to find Risc-Um had such a soft spoft. He had never suspected it.

"A tough meets a pretty face who turns him to butter and melts him down," Sey-Us replied, and chuckled. This turned Risc-Um indignant.

"It's not like that. Have I ever run out on you?" Sey-Us shook his head, pleased he had made his point.

"You've never lacked courage. But I've always thought of you as tough, Risc-Um, and now I find a dent in your armor. If Ihand-A can get to you…" Sey-Us shrugged angering Risc-Um.

"What are you driving at?" He reached out and clasped Risc-Um's shoulder.

"I'm teasing you to make a point. I'm glad Ihand-A and you are getting along. I know you'll be looking out for her and that will give me time to concentrate on work."

"Why do I feel so apprehensive about our destination? What are you going after, Sey-Us?"

"A legend a little like you, Risc-Um. This legend was a real brute, tougher than anyone. He would take on the world, whip anybody single-handed. Then one day, he came across a vision of loveliness. When he saw her he forgot how tough he was." Sey-Us paused looking thoughtful and looked at the sky.

"He forgot the hard code he lived by and that was when his enemies ganged up on him and brought him down. That's something to consider, Risc-Um." He regarded Sey-Us in silence wondering what he was talking about.

A young sailor came briskly up to them and stopped facing Sey-Us.

"What is it, Unbey?" Risc-Um asked. He glanced at him.

"The captain wants Dr. Sey-Us and you to come to the chart room. He said we've reached the position Dr. Sey-Us indicated on the map." Risc-Um glanced at Sey-Us then nodded and the sailor hurried away.

"This is what you've been waiting to hear, Risc-Um. Now I'll reveal what I'm after and where it is." They walked off toward the bridge.

They found Mai-Us spreading the map on the table. He was tranquil even at the moment of anticipated disclosure. He had laid out the most detailed chart of the Forgetten Zone they had. Sey-Us looked to Risc-Um.

"Ask Ihand-A to come up here, Risc-Um, I want you all to hear this."

She came on the bridge and looked to Sey-Us with an excited expression.

"It will be a relief to get this off my chest," Sey-Us said.

"This was our position half an hour ago, Sey-Us," Mai-Us said,
pointing to the map. "One degree north, one-fifty-three west. You promised us information on our destination when we reached this point." Mai-Us looked at Sey-Us expecting an answer. Risc-Um leaned against the table his fingers on the edge of the map. Sey-Us looked over the map and glanced at each of them.

"We're far west of Brutra," Sey-Us said, seemingly to himself, while he moved a finger across the map. He felt an electric excitement. This was the moment he had waited for – almost to a legend he had come to conquer.

"Very far west," Mai-Us said, glancing at Risc-Um. He had never seen Sey-Us so preoccupied, and during this voyage he hadn't been his normal self.

56

Whatever he was going after this time had brought about a marked change in Sey-Us.

"We're far from any waters I've sailed," Mai-Us said, briskly. "I can read the Smophes like my hand, but I've been in this area before."

"Which way do we go from here?" Risc-Um asked, impatiently.

"South by southwest," Sey-Us replied, with subdued excitement.

"What!" Mai-Us exclaimed, trying to figure out where the new course would take them. "There's nothing there but thousands of miles of ocean. What are we to do about food and fresh water? Having a larger crew makes those items critical." Mai-Us was determined to know more before he ordered the No'mo any further.

"Easy, Skipper," Sey-Us said, gently. He smiled as he drew his shoulders up, his face expressing an excitement he could barely contain.

"We won't be sailing more than another day from this position," Sey-Us said, taking an envelope from his pocket. He lifted the flap and removed a paper that he unfolded. It was a worn, taped map that he lay on the chart. Mai-Us, Risc-Um, and Ihand-A stared at the map as Sey-Us tapped it with a finger.

"This is the island we're bound for." Mai-Us leaned over the larger chart, studied it for a moment, and looked at Sey-Us. Calm as ever, Mai-Us felt some misgiving at the map of Sey-Us' island.

"I don't see it on the chart, Sey-Us," Mai-Us said.

"You won't find Scumm Island on any chart, Skipper," Sey-Us said, confidently. "It's never been charted. All we have to go on is my map. It and the position of the island was made by a Chimp skipper who sailed these waters three years ago."

"He must have been pulling your leg," Risc-Um said.

"He had to be," Mai-Us agreed. "It's impossible for an island that
size not be on charts. It couldn't have gone this long without someone discovering it." Sey-Us regarded Mai-Us with confidence.

"You're overlooking the obvious, Skipper," Sey-Us said. "This is the Forgotten Zone. There's little shipping in this area." Sey-Us was determined to convince them of the authenticity of his map. This was the decisive moment and Sey-Us reveled at such events.

"Of course there's no shipping," Mai-Us responded. "There's no place in this area to trade with." Sey-Us decided to tell them how he came to possess his map.

"A praho with natives from this island was blown out to sea. When the Chimp skipper found them, only one was still alive. Before he died, the Chimp skipper was able to get a description of the island and a fairly good idea of its location."

"How did you come to have the map?" Risc-Um asked. Mai-Us cut a slice of fruit and slipped it in his mouth.

"Just after we returned from the Northern Expedition, the Chimp
skipper brought it to me at the University. He had heard of me and felt I might be interested."

"This captain believed the native's story?" Mai-Us asked, ambivilant about the story and map. He recalled that others had disbelieved Sey-Us too, and had been shown up as fools. Sey-Us spread his hands.

"Why would a dying native lie to a benefactor?" Sey-Us countered. "I believe the story. I've researched it and turned my report into the Institute. Now we're here just about at the end of our voyage." Mai-Us shook his head.

"This could be a wild goose chase, Sey-Us," Mai-Us said, in a neutral tone.

"Skipper, I feel a map as detailed as this could not have been contrived from someone's imagination." Sey-Us' tone expressed conviction. Mai-Us silently agreed the map was remarkably detailed. As he and Risc-Um studied the map, they concurred with Sey-Us. At the left of the yellowed, frayed paper was a sandy peninsula. In front of it was a reef with a narrow passageway indicated in a light line. At the other side was a steep precipice that Sey-Us pointed to.

"According to the Chimp's notes, this cliff is over six hundred feet high and covered with dense jubgle. Here in the center upland is a mountain." Sey-Us paused as they looked at the outline of a shrivelled apple.

"This is the most curious aspect of the island," Sey-Us continued.
"A wall forty feet high stretches from one side of the peninsula to the other. It appears to be a barrier to whatever is on the other side." It was a disconcerting enigma to those looking at it. Mai-Us glanced at Sey-Us.

"Is that wall for real?" Mai-Us asked, incredulous. Sey-Us nodded.

"And what a wall, Skipper," Sey-Us said. "Built so long ago the descendants of the builders have slipped back to savagery. They've forgotten the remarkable civilization that erected the shield they depend on. That wall is as strong today as it was ages ago." He could see they were now accepting what he already knew. A little more convincing would win them over.

"The natives take care that wall never grows weak. They need it. But against what I have only the vaguest idea."

"The natives on these islands are Gorillas," Mai-Us said.

"And you can't convince me they were ever civilized enough to build a wall like that." Risc-Um passed a wry smile to Mai-Us. Both felt Sey-Us was chasing a rainbow this time.

"Maybe the Gorillas didn't build the wall," Ihand-A said. "They may have inherited it. There's evidence that an early civilization flourished here on Ephis. It seems that whatever threatened them still threatens the natives today, so they keep the wall in repair." All attention was on her.

"What I mean is, there's something on the other side of the wall the natives fear greatly. That fear is enough for them to keep the wall strong to keep whatever it is from their village." Mai-Us shook his head.

"We've come all this way for an unknown?" Mai-Us asked.

"Why are we here?" Risc-Um asked, more curious than ever to know why Sey-Us had behaved as he had on this voyage.

"I intend to find out what's on the other side of that wall," Sey-Us replied. "That's the purpose of this expedition." Mai-Us emitted an annoyed snort.

"A tribe of fierce enemies, more than likely," Mai-Us said, speculating. Now Risc-Um was feeling the excitement Sey-Us projected.

"If it was only another tribe, Skipper, why have the wall across the peninsula?" Risc-Um asked. "Another tribe could simply come around in prahos. Why is it so tall? A rival tribe doesn't make sense." It was now Risc-Um trying to fathom the riddle of the wall. Sey-Us knew he had convinced Risc-Um and looked to Mai-Us with anticipation. He raised the envelope and took out another sheet of paper but didn't unfold it.

"Have either of you heard of Gnok?" Sey-Us asked, in a serious tone. Risc-Um shook his head. Mai-Us chewed on a piece of fruit for a moment and turned his eyes to Sey-Us.

"Gnok did you say?" Mai-Us asked. Sey-Us nodded.

"Isn't it an island superstition?" Mai-Us asked. "A god, demon, something like that?"

"Well it's certainly something," Sey-Us agreed, opening the sheet of paper. "I don't believe it to be a god or demon, but something monsterous, powerful, and terribly alive, holding that island in the grip of mortal fear. Just as it held those intelligent ancestors who built the wall for their own safety." As Mai-Us slipped another slice of fruit into his mouth, a cold feeling of unease grew in Risc-Um. He felt Sey-Us had no right to be taking Ihand-A into such an unknown situation. Ihand-A accepted Sey-Us' explanation and started trying to reason an answer for the wall.

"I tell you, Skipper," Sey-Us said. "There's something on that island no civilized Orang has ever seen." He was conveying the idea of a lurking danger on Scumm Island, but knew Mai-Us was too realistic to accept what he said without proof.

"Every legend has some basis in truth and I don't think there's anything different about this," Sey-Us went on. "This island legend is no exception. I researched everything I could find about it." Mai-Us turned a calm look to Sey-Us.

"And you intend to study it!" Mai-Us exclaimed, in a flash of emotion unusual for him.

"If there's anything on that island worth studying, you bet I'm going to study it," Sey-Us said, firmly. "I've waited two years to get to that island and exploit any opportunity that comes my way."

"Suppose it doesn't want to be studied by you or anyone?" Risc-Um asked, in a dry tone. He was becoming uneasier the more he heard from Sey-Us.

Sey-Us smiled and rubbed his hands. Now he would give them the first clue as to his real intension.

"Suppose it doesn't? That's why I brought the vapor bombs. I've studied everything I could lay my hands on about the legend and the islands in this area. I feel certain I know the truth, at least what's based on established facts." Sey-Us turned his eyes to the open hatch. Soon now, he thought.

"What facts?" Risc-Um asked, bluntly. "If this island has never
been discovered, how can anything be known about it?" Sey-Us
turned his face to Risc-Um.

"There are similar legends on the known islands," Sey-Us replied. "I believe they all have one origin. I corroborated the facts and came up with a theory. From what I knew of the Chimp's story, this map, and the established facts, Scumm Island is the origin of the legend."

Still a bit skeptical, and anxious for Ihand-A, Risc-Um couldn't help turning his eyes to the sea also. In spite of himself, he felt a restless inner excitement as he recalled what had happened on previous expeditions. Mai-Us, chewing stoically, considered the small map and picked up a compass and began to mark it on the chart spread over the table. He knew how satisfied Sey-Us would be if he could prove that one legend was a living reality.

High above the No'mo's deck, Risc-Um pushed up the cover of the crow's nest and climbed through. He turned and extended a hand to Ihand-A and helped her up. His darker furred hand closed around
her light fur gently. When she stood beside him, he pushed the cover shut with a foot. They swayed slowly in the tranquil loft. At this height, they could feel the slight breeze.

Ihand-A pushed fur from her ears to let every part of her face receive the slight but welcome breeze. Risc-Um wiped his moist forehead.

From this vantagepoint, the ocean seemed more gray than blue, a play of light. Miles to the south, something resembling a vaporous cord stretched along the horizon, its ends disappearing in the distance. Risc-Um thought it a low cloud, but it soon appeared far too low for that. His mind began seeking a solution. It looked no higher than a finger's width above the water and projected gray wispy tendrils. Against the sweep of the sky, a bird glided easily and suddenly dove toward the sea. When it soared back up it carried a fish in its talons. It curved and glided, a splotch of red and black feathers that flew away with its catch. Except for the blotch, the secne was of a subtle blending of colors.

"How sublime," Ihand-A said, softly, as she turned completely around. She stopped with her eyes on Risc-Um.

"Why haven't you brought me up here before? Now I really feel like an explorer." He smiled and rubbed his chin.

"Let me see, an explorer is someone who gets someplace before anyone else. In that sense, you are an explorer." She got a puzzled look.

"How do you mean?"

"You're the only female to ever grace the crow's nest with your
charmn, and it seems natural for you to be here." He felt cheerful noting how her eyes gleamed with an inner intensity. After a moment of silence, Ihand-A saw the gray thread on the horizon.

"What's that? A cloud?" she asked, staring at the puff setting on the sea.

"Most likely. I noticed it when we first got up here." His mind kept puzzling over the vaporous string on the ocean.

It appeared stationary while at the same time would suddenly send a spiral into the sky.

"Just think of it, Risc-Um. Here we are sailing for an island where we'll all be explorers. The first to land there! It's provacative. When do you think we'll reach the island?" Her eager, inquiring eyes met his for a moment before he looked away.

"If there is an island, we better find it in the next couple of days. Sey-Us' one day sailing from the coordinates have become two and a half days." He got a smile as he looked at her. He felt less apprehensive since they hadn't found the island. At least, not where Sey-Us had thought it was. Risc-Um was beginning to believe Sey-Us had been fooled by the Chimp and had been naïve for trusting someone he didn't know. It was such a wild story, yet he half hoped there was an island to be found. He could use some excitement. He knew Ihand-A had picked up her eagerness from Sey-Us and was hoping she wouldn't be disappointed.

"Dr. Sey-Us is so tense about the error in the island's location he can't seem to stand still," she said, abruptly interrupting his thoughts. "I don't think he was able to sleep and he's very cranky."

"I'm sort of disappointed myself, and a little nervous." He turned his eyes back to the strange form on the sea and got a very unsettling feeling. Ihand-A was giving him a cold look. It surprised Risc-Um at how quickly her mood could change.

"You're disappointed? I thought you didn't believe there was an island." Her mocking tone stung.

"I hope there isn't," he said, somberly. She quickly folded her arms and gave him a hard look.

"As I recall, you were the one who fled from a warm, safe world to find a life of adventure." Her tone became softly teasing, but her words still cut him the wrong way.

Risc-Um couldn't find a way to defend himself on his vacilating position about the island. He wavered between relief at not finding it and discouragement. If Ihand-A had any suspicion as to his motive for not wanting to find Scumm Island, she didn't give it away.

Risc-Um knew none of them had any conception of what they might find on the island. He had to convey his uneasiness to her.

"Sey-Us takes too many foolish risks. I know, I've seen him in action. I'm worried about what he might expect from you."

"After what he's done for me, I'll do whatever he asks. I owe him that. Knowing me, Risc-Um, would you expect any less? He has more consideration than you give him credit for." He was helpless before her loyalty.

"You don't understand, Ihand-A. He couldn't care less what happens to who as long as he makes discoveries no one else would dare tackle." He quickly held up a hand.

"I know what you're going to say. He would never ask any of us to do anything he wouldn't do. But as far as I'm concerned, that applies to males and that's what makes this situation different. I'm worried about you."

"You needn't be. I'll do that," she snapped.

"Did Sey-Us tell you what might be on that island?" She gave him an angry glare.

"He told me what he believes about this Gnok. Get this clear, Risc-Um. I can take care of myself. I've faced things in Icense far worse than anything we can possibly find here in the Forgotten Zone." After her outburst, she turned her back on him. He put his hand on her arm.

"I can't help it, Ihand-A If anything should happen to you… Please look at me." He was pleading , hoping for her common sense to rule, not her gratitude to Sey-Us.

He was surprised that Sey-Us had told her more than he had told Mai-Us and himself. Mai-Us was very perceptive noting Sey-Us was treating her like a daughter. After all the time Risc-Um had spent with her, he didn't understand her any better. She stubbornly kept her back to him. He looked at an ear with a golden wisp of fur curling behind it. He felt she was acting childish but determined not to give up on her.

"I care for you, Ihand-A." She still wouldn't look at him, but his words made her turn her eyes down. He put his hands on her shoulders and drew her against him. For a brief time she didn't resist. Realizing what he was doing, she twisted away from his hands and stepped away from him.

"Look at me," he said, desperate. "There may be little time before we reach the island. I'm afraid for you, and frightened of you. I care for you. Haven't you anything to say about that?" She turned, stepped forward, and pressed against him. Risc-Um got a hopeful smile.

Sunset was near and the sky was flooded with a cacophony of subtle colors and tints that blended with and danced on the waves. Once again, an elegant bird soared in the prismatic sky and was lost in the glare. To the south, the vague cottony cord had been growing into a wall of fog that seemed to be moving toward the No'mo. Ihand-A and Risc-Um were too interested in each other to note the growing phenomena approaching as they walked the deck holding hands.

As the No'mo pushed along at twenty-two knots, the ominous, thick gray-white cloud slowly swirled above the water in the fading light. Later, the fog would swallow the No'mo.

SCUMM ISLAND

As the dark hours passed, the fog thickened and Mai-Us cut the No'mo's speed by half. It was three hours after sunrise before there was enough of a diffuse glow to move about without a flashlight. Before the first dim rays of the sun penetrated the fog, the ship steered by Mai-Us, was closing with the island. He had again reduced speed as they were sailing in unknown waters in a dense fog.

The clock on the bridge showed noon but the deck still looked like a half-hour after sunrise. The No'mo was inching along through a fog bank that seemed to have no end. Against the invading moisture of the mist, no garment was spared. Everyone's clothing hung in loose, soggy folds. Water condensed everywhere and dripped off anything high enough to allow gravity to work. It clung tenaciously to the fur of the crew making them miserable. It condensed on masts and, bulkheads, and on the hard wooden deck moving along in sluggish, twisted rivulets.

At a distance of a few feet, sailors, masts and air vents became vague, shadowy specters. No more than six feet away they would vanish ghost-like into the damp stillness. The No'mo sailed on for another hour and still found no end to the fog. On the bridge, Mai-Us held the wheel steady as he carefully kept a watch on the compass. Sey-Us, Risc-Um, and Ihand-A strained their eyes looking into the fog but couldn't see the sailor who manned the sounding line at the bow. Another sailor, in the crow's nest, could see nothing but fog surrounding the ship. The sailor with the sounding line could be heard on the bridge. By some freak of atmospherics, his voice seemed to carry more loudly than in clear weather. It felt as if the ship was sailing in a box that held in sound and amplified it. Sey-Us, as usual, was impatient.

"Flaming hell! Isn't this fog ever going to end?" he said. He was as tense as a person standing atop a volcano and not knowing when it would erupt. He stared into the cloaking cloud as if he might miss something if he glanced away.

"Are you certain of our position, Mai-Us?" Sey-Us asked, without turning.

"Positive," Mai-Us replied, calmly. He leaned against the wheel and cut a slice of fruit and took a bite. Putting his hands back on the wheel, he enlightened Sey-Us.

"Before we ran into this fog, I got a true bearing and checked it twice against opposing stars. There's no mistake about our position. I've been keeping a close watch on our speed and calculating distance." Ihand-A took hold of Risc-Um's hand and he felt her excitement.

"If we don't get out of this fog soon, I'm going to burst with

anticipation," she said. "I've never been this excited and I'm loving it." She didn't see the disappointed look Risc-Um cast at her.

"Don't be so optimistic," Risc-Um said. "And don't stand so close to the railing. You know the deck is slippery." He held tightly to her hand knowing more talk would be good for both of them.

"I'm ready to pop like a squeezed grape," he admitted. "I feel like diving over the side and swimming ahead to see the island." She looked at him with an enthusiastic smile.

"I'm glad you feel that way," she said. They regarded each other for a few seconds before he frowned.

"When I think of what we might be taking you into, I want to turn this ship around." Ihand-A quickly turned an annoyed look to him.

"Stop worrying about me. I'm part of the expedition. Relax, if that's possible." Her tone held no anger, only determination.

"If our position is correct, I can see why the Chimp skipper made the error on the location of the island," Sey-Us said. "That being so, we should be close to the island." He, too, was ready to get started after his long wait. Standing in the fog, Sey-Us felt triumphant and could hardly wait to set foot on Scumm Island.

"We could sail past it in this fog," Risc-Um said. Sey-Us hadn't thought of that as he glanced at Risc-Um

"If we don't sight the island after this fog lifts, then it doesn't

exist," Mai-Us said. Sey-Us noted a trace of excitement in Mai-Us'

voice as he kept a calm exterior.

"We have to land soon, Sey-Us, or be forced to turn back," Mai-Us reminded him. The tense voice of the sailor with the sounding line came to them.

"Bottom one-twenty-five."

"The Chimp was making an educated guess at the island's position," Sey-Us said, hopefully. "I thought he had been closer to it."

"How will we know it's the right island?" Ihand-A asked, realizing quickly she had made a mistake.

"The shriveled apple mountain," Sey-Us snapped. He pushed his vision into the fog as his impatience became almost unbarable, and not just for him.

"I'm sorry," Ihand-A said, smarting at the rebuke. "It slipped my mind."

"Bottom eighty," came the disembodied voice from the bow. They all tensed for the next call, and didn't have long to wait.

"Bottom seventy-five." Sey-Us rubbed his hands savoring the moment.

"It's shallowing fast," Mai-Us said, gripping the wheel against an impact on a reef. "Bring her to dead slow, Risc-Um." Dead slow was rang up on the annunciator and immediately answered. The No'mo had slowed so its forward motion was a controlled drift.

"The fog seems to be thinning," Ihand-A said, noting the growing brightness. The others, gazing into the fog, hadn't seemed to have heard her.

"Bottom at sixty-five."

"What's the No'mo's draft?" Sey-Us asked, concerned the ship might strike the reef that appeared on the map.

"Twenty feet," Mai-Us replied, alert to Sey-Us' concern. Through the fog came a sound that was slow to register on anyone's consciousness until Ihand-A picked up on it.

"What's that noise?" she asked. Though faint, it now throbbed in her ears. Sey-Us gave her a puzzled look.

"What is it you hear?" Sey-Us asked, still unaware of the sound. She shook her head.

"I'm not sure," she replied, turning her head, unable to identify the sound. The others caught the faint sound and listened. From the crow's nest came an excited shout.

"Breakers."

"Where away?" Risc-Um shouted, through cupped hands.

"Dead ahead." Risc-Um turned quickly and rang stop. The dying throbs of the engines were heard before the engine room complied.

The No'mo glided out of the fog into sunshine.

"Bottom at fifty," the now visible sailor called, pulling in the sounding line.

"Drop anchor," Mai-Us ordered. The chains clanked and rattled through the hawser guides on the bow. The anchors splashed into the water on their way to the bottom.

The No'mo was motionless and quiet, resting in the sunshine as the crew made her secure. All could clearly hear the sound rolling over the sea like a wave.

"That's not breakers," Risc-Um said.

"It's drums," Mai-Us said, in a level voice. Sey-Us' eyes turned back to the fog. It lay aft and on the horizon. He noted his companions staring he turned back and saw an island as duplicated on his map. Ihand-A became aware that the ship was silent.

"I knew it was here," Sey-Us said. The black rock of the island
contrasted with the verdant green foliage on the upper slope of the
island. Sey-Us turned again to the fog.

"Amazing!" Sey-Us exclaimed. They all turned and looked at the wall of fog that lay on the horizon encircling the island.

"A perpetuating ring of fog," Sey-Us said, awed. "Look at it will you. I've never seen such a phenomena."

"You really think it's perpetual, Sey-Us?" Mai-Us asked. The experience of awe filled Sey-Us as he watched the fog swirl and dance above the water.

"I've never heard of a ring of fog or an enduring fog bank," Sey-Us replied. "But there's so much we don't understand about the Forgotten Zone." He looked to Mai-Us.

"Anything's possible, Skipper."

"This explains why the island has remained undiscovered," Ihand-A said.

"You're right," Sey-Us said, in a complementary tone.

"Look over there, Dr. Sey-Us," she said, excited. In the distance, standing tall a thick jugle stood at the base of the shriveled mountain. It was black against the sky and birds could be seen soaring over the island.

Their harsh cries could be vaguely heard as they dived through the mist that spread across the crown of the bleak, rugged peaks.

The island reached out to the ship with long sparsely covered finger of shimmering white sand and sooty, russet rocks. The peninsula was little different from the one on the map. The Chimp had a good head for detail, never having been to the island, Sey-Us thought. He turned to Risc-Um and Mai-Us with a triumphant expression.

"What do you think of my map now?" Risc-Um and Mai-Us exchanged pleased looks knowing Sey-Us always seemed to be proven right.

"There's the wall," Sey-Us said, clasping Mai-Us' shoulder and pointing. "Can you see it, Skipper?" Sey-Us had been waiting a long time for this moment of vindication. Sey-Us bolted from the bridge, half climbing half sliding down to the deck shouting excitedly.

"Make ready the boats. Prepare to lower away." Mai-Us caught up with him and got him calmed down, explaining they would have to change clothes before embarking for the island.

Risc-Um and Ihand-A returned to the bridge and stood looking at the island.

"It seems so strange. Have you ever saw anything like it, Risc-Um?" He saw she was fascinated at the spectacle the island presented. The excitement quickly drained from him as he watched her. His jaw tightened and he walked from the bridge without answering her. She stared after him, confused at his action. He went to direct the stocking and lowering of the boats. Sey-Us came rushing to a boat that was being loaded with rifles and ammunition. Ihand-A followed him, stepping quickly to keep up and stopping beside Sey-Us.

"You are letting me come with you, aren't you, Dr. Sey-Us?" she asked, afraid of being left on the ship. He patted her arm with a confident look.

"Of course, my dear. One cannot function properly without one's aide." He turned back to the boat and Ihand-A was satisfied. Risc-Um heard them and came to the boat.

"I don't think it's good idea to take her ashore, Sey-Us. At least, until we have some idea of what we might run into." He knew his words weren't impressing Sey-Us.

"Nonsense, Risc-Um, I've learned to always keep my tools and aides with me. I never know when I might need them. Since this is my expedition, allow me to run it as I see fit." Sey-Us spoke in a strong, authoritative voice, and Risc-Um tried to reason with him.

"Sey-Us, it's crazy to risk…" He half turned toward Ihand-A hoping for support. Instead, he found her glaring angrily at him.

"Butt out, Mr. First Mate," she said, barely concealing her anger. He knew reason wasn't going to work and turned back to Sey-Us.

"Make certain the other boat is correctly loaded, Risc-Um," Sey-Us said, tersely. "And make certain everyone going ashore has a rifle and ammunition. Put a case of vapor bombs in this boat and assign crew to carry my equipment. I want to get ashore before dark." Risc-Um wavered for a moment and with a helpless shrug, and disapproving look from Ihand-A, he turned to the crew and began spouting orders. Sey-Us shook his head and gave Ihand-A a mischievous wink. She looked quickly away, embarrassed that he knew of the relationship between Risc-Um and her. She realized anyone could see it when they were together.

"Send someone to get your field kit, Ihand-A," Sey-Us said, firmly. "You go in the boat with Risc-Um.

That will placate him and make him feel he's protecting you."

"I'll get my kit, Doctor." He smiled as she moved away. Any of his other aides wouldn't have hesitated to send one of the crew. But Ihand-A was special.

Sey-Us ventured back to the bridge where Mai-Us was scanning
the shore with binoculars.

"See anything interesting, Skipper?" Mai-Us kept the binoculars to his eyes as he shook his head.

"There are a few huts at the edge of the foliage above the peninsula. Other than that, nothing." Sey-Us glanced at him puzzled by his tone.

"You sound worried, Mai-Us. What is it?" Mai-Us lowered the binoculars and turned his face to him.

"There's not a sign of life, and that's enough to worry me, Sey-Us. This is the first island I've put into where the whole population didn't show up to look us over, and those natives were familiar with ships. If we're the first to visit here I feel this bodes ill. I don't like it at all."

"The natives might be too busy to bother with us. Listen to those drums, Mai-Us. They must be having some sort of ritual. By the way, when I was looking from the bow, I'm certain I saw some large structures back where the trees are thicker. Can you see anything?" Mai-Us raised the binoculars and turned them in the direction Sey-Us had indicated.

"I can't make out anything. The trees block the view." Sey-Us nodded. They stood quiet listening to the raw, savage rhythm of the drums swell and fall. It was a deep, steady thunder rolling across the serene water. Gradually, it melded into a fast paced, urgent beat reaching a crescendo.

It pulsed in primal cadence through them. Shaking his head, Mai-Us lowered the binoculars but kept his eyes on the beach.

"It seems strange they haven't noticed our arrival," Mai-Us said, trying to resolve the natives' lack of interest. "They should be crowding the beach. I've never known any native who wasn't curious when a ship put in at their island." Sey-Us and Mai-Us regarded the empty beach for a silent moment, then Mai-Us looked to Sey-Us and pointed to the island.

"Every aborigine should be on that beach. I tell you, Sey-Us, this isn't normal behavior." Mai-Us had an uneasy feeling and was bewildered at his lack of interest.

"It's possible they haven't seen us," Sey-Us said. "Maybe they have and those are signaling drums." Even as he spoke, Sey-Us knew better. Mai-Us regarded him for a moment.

"Those are ceremonial drums. You're familiar with island drums, Sey-Us. You can tell by the tempo the difference between a signal and a ritual beat. Those drums are for some ceremony inland far enough to have kept them from seeing us. And by the sound, it must be big magic."

"At least, we won't have any problem landing," Sey-Us said. Mai-Us shook his head.

"This is a bad situation, Sey-Us. You know how touchy islanders can be about their rituals." Mai-Us spoke in a calm voice. He felt that to show fear in front of the crew would set a bad example for a captain and undermine his authority.

Mai-Us and Sey-Us came to Risc-Um who was superving a boat.

"Where's the boatswain?" Mai-Us asked, loudly. A thickset Chimp stepped to the boat.

"Yes, Captain?" he asked, gruffly.

"I'm leaving you in charge," Mai-Us said. "Secure the ship and set a sharp watch." Mai-Us turned to Risc-Um.

"Select the men for your boat," Mai-Us said. "I've got a bad feeling about this and want to be ready if we run into trouble." Risc-Um had learned through experience that if the skipper smelled trouble there was usually lots of it.

Risc-Um gathered the crew and began calling out the names of those who would go in his boat. When Pablae didn't hear his name called, he gave the first mate a look of disappointment. Risc-Um smiled and shook his head.

"Who's going to carry the vapor bombs?" Sey-Us asked. Risc-Um
pointed to a young Orang.

"Thespa, you go in the boat with the doctor," Risc-Um ordered. Thespa bent to the wooden case, hefted it slightly, and looked indignant at its weight. He lifted it without complaint and handed it to another sailor in the boat, climbed in, and secured the case.

"You're coming, aren't you, Skipper?" Sey-Us asked. "Never know when you might be able to help." Risc-Um knew the answer before Sey-Us had asked.

"I've never missed setting foot on an island once sailing to it," Mai-Us replied. "Besides, someone has to keep your enthuaiasm under control." Sey-Us laughed and patted Mai-Us' shoulder.

"You might have to be our interpreter," Sey-Us said. "That might be vital."

"The boats are ready, Skipper," Risc-Um reported.

Mai-Us and Sey-Us climbed down the rope ladder into the boat and Mai-Us ordered it away. Risc-Um was waiting for Ihand-A. She came hurrying along with the field kit dangling from her shoulder. She now determined to show Risc-Um just how tough she was.

She took the strap from her shoulder, leaned over the railing, and dropped the kit to a sailor. She took hold of the rope ladder and quickly climbed down followed by Risc-Um. Once everyone was seated, Risc-Um ordered the boat away.

As they rowed toward the island, Risc-Um ordered the only precaution he could think of.

"Everybody load your rifles and fill a pocket with extra ammo. After you in the stern do so, relieve the rowers so they can load up. We've got to be ready for the unexpected." He watched as each of the crew took their turn at an oar. He looked at Ihand-A with a glum expression, not knowing what to say after her refusal to support him. Eventually, she broke the silence between them.

"This is the first time I've seen so many of the crew together," she said. "I hadn't thought there were so many." She gave him a hopeful look wondering if he would pick up on it. But he had no idea what he could say.

"Look at this landing party," she continued. "There are fifteen in each boat."

"And we might need everyone of them on the island," Risc-Um said. He had been hoping for something more, but it didn't come.

"The natives will probably be as friendly as children. I sware, Risc-Um, you're such a pessimist."

"Children? That's a good one," he replied. "Hear those drums? I believe there's some sort of ritual going on. I only wish we knew what kind before we go butting in. Natives tend to get mighty upset at having outsiders see their magic." He felt somewhat better now that he had told her what they might face. But Ihand-A wasn't to be deterred.

"Sounds like a wedding to me," she said, making light of the savage tempo.

Risc-Um stared in disbelief. It was hard for him to believe she could be so naïve about the danger they might face.

"I knew a couple of sailors who spied on a native ceremony," he said, grimly. "Their bones are still on the beach of that island." Risc-Um hoped that would shock her, but was proven wrong. He watched her fur gently rippling around her face. What a sucker I am, he thought. But he had perked her curiosity.

"Had they interfered with the native ceremony?" she asked. He shook his head.

"Just hid and watched. They got spears in their backs for it." She
gasped and said nothing more. He turned his eyes back to the No'mo's crows nest and saw her look too. She looked at him with a pleased expression.

The volume of the drums grew with each pull on the oars. The rhythm altered and became distinctly different, sounding too awesome for a simple ritual. When the rhythm changed, it chilled Risc-Um and filled him with cold dread. He had to face reality knowing the crew knew the risk they were taking. It was what they done for a living and each had signed on for this trip. Not so Ihand-A, he thought. Sey-Us has impressed her.

Mai-Us was checking to make sure the boat was safely on the beach while Sey-Us was puttering with a camera whose strap hung around his neck. The sailors pulled hard on the oars through the shallow surf until Risc-Um's boat grounded on the beach. Mai-Us waited for Risc-Um while Sey-Us took some shots of the fog. It was an amazing sight to him. In all his voyages into the unknown, he had never encountered such a phenomenon.

After a few moments, Sey-Us turned and burdened a sailor with his rifle, another with ammunition, and a third with the rest of his equipment.

As he done this, Mai-Us was handing out ammunition to the sailors. Thespa showed annoyance as he shouldered the case of vapor bombs and stepped beside Sey-Us.

"Stay close to me, Thespa," Sey-Us said. "And watch your step.
There's enough Trithonol gas in those bombs to put everybody on this island to sleep for a week."

"I'll be extra careful," Thespa said, suddenly feeling the importance of his task. "Do you think we're going to run into something you might have to use these on?" Sey-Us gave him a serious look.

"I'm counting on it," Sey-Us replied. "And if I'm lucky, it will take more than one of them to knock it out." Thespa stared at him dumbfounded. Veterans who had sailed with Sey-Us before had told Thespa of some of the tight pinches Sey-Us had gotten them into. As he recalled those tales, his throat became dry. Sey-Us turned.

"Where's Risc-Um? I want my aide at my side." Risc-Um took Ihand-A by the arm and joined Sey-Us. The boats had been secured on the beach.

"Leave an armed hand with each boat, Risc-Um," Sey-Us said.

"Already taken care of," Risc-Um said, as Sey-Us took hold of Ihand-A's arm.

"Stay close to me and Risc-Um, my dear."

"I'll watch out for her," Risc-Um declared. Sey-Us shook his head and chuckled. The exultation he had felt at the first sight of the island had abated and Sey-Us was again indomitable and quick with tolerance.

"Very well, Risc-Um, I'll leave her in your capable hands. But guard her well and make certain she's close in case I need her assistance." Sey-Us looked to Mai-Us.

"Are we ready to go, Mai-Us?"

Mai-Us nodded and signaled the others into forming a double column that moved unevenly along the beach toward the native village and the sound of the drums.

Sey-Us took the lead striding vigorously toward the village with Thespa right beside him. Mai-Us and Risc-Um were at the head of the columns and Ihand-A was beside Ric-Um walking fast to keep up. They trooped away from the beach and up a small elevation. When the wall came into view it took on an immense proportion, although they were still a good distance from it. The Chimp skipper's sketch had poorly estimated the mighty barrier that ran the width of the peninsula. Sey-Us was quick to note that it wasn't forty feet tall but a staggering sixty. It was constructed with black and gray stones with white veins of some mineral embedded in them. Brush closed on its base as did jutting trees.

Sey-Us saw the wall's vastness seemed dwarfed by the black
mountain on its far side. Along the wall lay brown logs and stacks of jungle vine. In its center was a great hinged gate connected on both sides by gray stone pillars that supported the wall's antiquity. It's hinges were made of iron embedd in the pillars. What surprised Sey-Us was that they were rust free.

They stopped for a few minutes to admire the majesty of the wall taking in what details they could see. The drumbeat increased snapping them back to reality. They slowly began to approach the huts, yet no native had been seen. Each of the yellow and green huts was deserted. No one appeared when the invaders passed toward the center of the village. They're certainly busy with their magic, Sey-Us thought. It appeared the whole tribe was taking part and that made him uneasy at their total lack of curiosity.

The size of the village indicated a complement of about a hundred members and all the huts were widely spaced and partailly masked by the thick brush. Only a narrow dirt path connected them. Each stood in the circle of bare earth beaten to a powdery dust by many feet over a long period of time.

To a point, it looked like any native village in the Forgotten Zone. The one extraordinary detail that made this village different was the broken stone pillars scattered among ruins that had been skillfully built. There were more ruins closer to the wall and presented an amazing sight. The ruins of an advanced but ancient civilization conjured questions for Sey-Us.

"From the looks of those ruins, it's my opinion this must have been an inner defense of a large city," Sey-Us said, pointing around at the broken columns. Ihand-A stared wide-eyed.

"But it's so huge, Dr. Sey-Us," Ihand-A said, awed, looking at the ruins.

"Stupendous," Mai-Us said. "These ruins are similar to the ancient ruins at Iscat."

"The ones in the eastern Forgotten zone, Skipper?" Risc-Um asked, comparing the markings on the columns. Mai-Us nodded.

"But those can't compare with these for size."

"Who could have built this place, Dr. Sey-Us?" Ihand-A asked, in a revernt tone.

"Not the presnt day inhabitants," Sey-Us replied. "We'll endeavor to discover the earlier inhabitants, if we can. Because of its age, that may not prove feasible." Sey-Us stepped to one of the columns and examined the strange symbols on its face. It felt extremely odd standing amid such ruins and hearing the ceaseless, primitive drums.

"We landed at Belpa once," Risc-Um said. "It's impressive too, but not the way this place is. Nobody has any idea who built it either." He knew these ruins made Belpa pale by comparision as the ruins awed him, too.

"What a discovery. I've got to get photographs of these magnificent ruins," Sey-Us said, turning to Ihand-A. "I need you to stand by these pillars so I can get a true scale of their size." Sey-Us was excited at the prospects such a discovery would afford him. He always liked discoveries he could shove in the faces of his colleagues. Yet the natives were still unaware of their presence.

Abruptly, the throb of the drums softened and voices could be heard swelling in a chant. Risc-Um quickly raised an arm for them to remain silent. Ihand-A and Sey-Us were too busy to notice the difference. The voices seemed to be coming from near the wall. Sey-Us stopped and listened. He motioned to Mai-Us and pointed to an unusually large hut on their right. Mai-Us understood and nodded the group toward the hut

"We should be able to see the natives once we clear this hut," Sey-Us said, in a low voice, that didn't befit his personality.

"Do you hear what thery're chanting?" Ihand-A asked, in an alarmed tone. Risc-Um was also intently listening.

"Why they're chanting Gnok, Gnok," Mai-Us said. "Can't you make it out, Sey-Us?"

"It must be some religious rite," Risc-Um said, growing uneasier by the minute. He sorely wished Ihand-A had remained onboard the No'mo.

"I hear them," Sey-Us said. "Let's move closer." Sey-Us glanced at the hands with a cautionary look.

"Be careful," Sey-Us warned, in a voice just audible. To Risc-Um, it seemed Sey-Us' warning was only an afterthought.

Moving forward warily, Sey-Us stopped and beckoned for Mai-Us, who moved forward and bent his head close to Sey-Us'.

"Do you understand their language?" Sey-Us whispered.

"I haven't heard enough to be certain," Mai-Us replied, and turned his head to listen. Risc-Um and Ihand-A stood behind them almost holding their breath.

"It sounds like a dialect similar to the Ulder Island natives," Mai-Us said. "But I can't be certain."

"Is it similar enough for you to communicate?" Sey-Us asked,
feeling excited again. Mai-Us turned an annoyed look to him.

"If you'll be quiet and let me listen, I'll let you know." Sey-Us shut up.

They stood at the corner of the hut, out of sight, but able to peer around it. Sey-Us turned and waved for the others to close up then peered around the hut. Mai-Us glanced at Sey-Us.

"I believe I can speak with them, Sey-Us." Sey-Us patted Mai-Us' shoulder.

"Good. Let's see all we can then conduct our meeting correctly. Everthing's going to depend on that." Sey-Us turned back to watching then glanced at Mai-Us.

"Wait here," Sey-Us said. "I'm going to see if I can find out what's going on." He slipped around the corner of the hut before anyone could say word.

Ihand-A stayed close to Risc-Um as he eyed the crew, measuring their degree of readiness. Mai-Us leaned against the hut and cut a slice of fruit. Sey-Us quickly reappeared, his eyes flashing
excitement.

"Mai-Us, Risc-Um, come with me. You've got to see this," he whispered, and moved back toward the center of the village. They moved toward the chanting, stopped, and Sey-Us raised his camera and began working it as fast as his finger could turn the film. They stood at the corner of a small hut and watched the bizarre ritual. The drums boomed out a steady, low throbbing note, above that could be heard the shouts of many voices expressing exultation followed by a cowing tone.

Irresistably drawn, the sailors moved forward until they stood clear of the screening hut staring in the direction of the chanters. Taking another step to the side, they saw a wide, smooth stone stage that ended against the wall. Looking at the gate, they saw it was held closed by an immense log pushed through metal hasps. Also visible was a low flight of gray steps half way across the plaza on a crude altar covered with palm fronds sat a young female aborigine. There could not have been found in any Gorilla tribe a female so attractive. A woven ribbon of yellow and purple flowers served as a tiara, sash, and collar was her only attire.

Sey-Us noted her tender, cowed allure and began feeling so strange that he quickly associated it with the scent of the flowers that permeated the area. On either side of the female, intoning natives chanted and swayed. To one side, but dominating by eye and posture, stood a black furred witch doctor convulsed in the ritualistic chaos. Behind him stood a veritable titan, gaudily garbed with colorful feathers watching over the ceremony with regal aloofness.

The natives were so engrossed that none had noticed the newly arrived staring group. The native show had a hypnotic fascination for them as they witnessed such raw savagery as was displayed before their eyes.

"Keep it up, you magnificent savages," Sey-Us mumbled, as he focused the camera. Swing, turn, aim, shoot was all he was concentrating on. Only the moment mattered to Sey-Us. As the others moved up with Sey-Us, Mai-Us, and Risc-Um they were engrossed by the spectacle. Stepping beside Sey-Us, Thespa noted the tall Gorilla.

"Who's the one in the feathered cape?" Thespa asked.

"The chief. Top of the totem around here," Sey-Us replied, without interrupting his picture taking.

The chief began an odd invocating pirouette toward the flower-
clad female. His hands moving in gestures that seemed to offer her to the nine tall dancers that leaped toward her. They wore fearsome heads with a white face and their bodies covered in white powder.

"Primaloids!" Mai-Us exclaimed, surprised. "Those nine are acting as primaloids, or something close. It appears they're acting out some sort of appeasement rite." This brought Sey-Us to look at Mai-Us.

"Flaming hell! I believe you're right, Mai-Us." Ihand-A shuddered beside Risc-Um as she thought about the sailors he had mentioned. She was frightened. But only a little, she thought.

Mai-Us abruptly turned and regarded Ihand-A, then deliberately moved to the side where he stood between her and the natives. Motivated by Mai-Us, the sailors pushed into a tighter group around her. When Ihand-A began to push them back and stand on tiptoe, Risc-Um intervened, as she was well screened.

The primaloid-like dancers pranced around the female and beat on their chests. The witch doctor stepped to the chief and made a gesture that Sey-Us felt meant it was his time to join the ritual. What part he was to play, the secret watchers were never to know.

As the witch doctor moved, the corner of his eye caught sight of Sey-Us and the others. He shouted something incoherent and pointed to the landing party.

The chanting, dancing, all sound and movement froze. The sudden
hush carried an overt threat. As no one on either side moved, it
seemed they had a standoff.

"Stay where you are," Sey-Us ordered. "Don't make any sudden moves. Let's see what they're going to do." The sailors reinforced their shield around Ihand-A. As tension rose, Mai-Us stepped in front of Sey-Us.

"This is the time for me to speak, Sey-Us. It may be our only chance to avoid a bloody encounter. The witch doctor called the ritual to a stop and said there were strangers watching, or something pretty close to that." The natives were sullenly glaring at the No'mo party. Then, as if by silent command, the females and children began melting away into the brush. A shiver ran Thespa's spine.

"They're clearing out," Thespa said, in a panicky tone. "We better get out of here." He spun toward the beach but Risc-Um seized his arm with a steel grip.

"No one's going anywhere just yet," Risc-Um said, firmly. "When we go we won't be running. That's the quickest way to get a spear in your back." For a moment, Thespa stared at Risc-Um and nodded. He understood that if he had run there would have been no chance of avoiding a fight. Thespa had heard of the savagery of island Gorillas. Infuriating them or showing your back was a good way to remain on an island permanently.

"Good thinking, Risc-Um," Sey-Us said. He stood boldly at the head of the landing party with Mai-Us.

"No use trying to conceal ourselves," Sey-Us said. "Everybody step slowly from the hut. It's time to bluff." Mai-Us glanced over his shoulder and spoke.

"Stick together and we'll come out of this." Sey-Us had kept his eyes on the chief who seemed to have made up his mind.

Raising his arm, he denoted two warriors who moved beside him. He began a slow walk toward the party as the last females and children slipped away. Only the warriors and witch doctor remained on the plaza along with the female on the altar. When Sey-Us looked at her, he saw her eyes were glazed and she made no effort to leave. He felt she was drugged.

As the chief and his guards neared, Thespa became more on edge.

"What's he trying to pull?" Thespa asked, alarmed.

"How would I know?" Sey-Us snapped. "Shut up and don't let them know you fear them." Sey-Us hadn't taken his eyes off the chief. The chief took one long deliberate step forward, stopped, and regarded them with an angry stare.

"Is there going to be trouble, Risc-Um?" Ihand-A asked, in a whisper. He glanced at her.

"It will be trouble for the natives if they start anything," he replied. "They've probably never heard gunfire." He squeezed her hand for reassurance.

The chief kept staring, trying to intimidate them. Sey-Us noted a look of caution come to him. Some of the sailors had shifted their rifles and slipped a nervous finger around the triggers. Sey-Us, as though he had seen them, spoke in a steady voice.

"Take it easy. The chief's a cautious one. There's nothing to be alarmed about."

"He's trying a bluff," Risc-Um explained. "He's waiting to see if we run. It's his game, but my money is on Sey-Us and the skipper." The sailors seemed to relax a little.

The stand off continued until one of the sailors spoke for them all.

"Talk to him, Captain. Make a friendly speech." Mai-Us stepped away from Sey-Us and faced the chief who jerked his arm up in warning. Mai-Us spoke, but no one in the landing party understood what he said.

"I've just greeted him and told him we were friends," Mai-Us said, without looking away from the chief. Mai-Us carried the conversation in two languages, speaking slowly and using deliberate gestures. The chief's eyes widened and he shouted scornfully.

"What's he saying, Mai-Us?" Sey-Us asked, impatient that Mai-Us wasn't keeping him up on the conversation. Sey-Us wanted to stay on top of the situation and avoid trouble.

"He says they need no friends and that we're to leave. We've brought evil magic," Mai-Us said, daring a glance at Sey-Us. "Evil that's disrupted their ceremony." Sey-Us thought quickly about how to handle this.

"Try to convince him to let us stay, and ask about the ceremony." Mai-Us began speaking in a placid, conciliatory tone as he pointed to the flower-draped female. She sat paying no attention to what was transpiring before her. Mai-Us also believed she was drugged. The chief waved his arm at her and spoke proudly.

"Gonk. Gnok," the warriors said, loudly in unison, in a worshipful tone.

"He says she's the bride of Gnok," Mai-Us said.

"Gnok!" Sey-Us exclaimed, jubilant.

Before anymore was said, the witch doctor vaulted forward, his
headdress shaking wildly and his dark eyes shooting fury at the chief. He was agitated and shrieked hysterically.

"What got into him?" Sey-Us asked, becoming uneasy.

"The witch doctor says the chief had better listen to him," Mai-Us replied. "He says the ceremony has been ruined because strange eyes have looked on their magic, and he's very angry."

"Try to calm him down, Mai-Us. What's their word for friend?" Sey-Us felt he needed to help out. Mai-Us glanced at him.

"Their word for friend is dera. Go easy, Sey-Us, or we'll have trouble. The witch doctor will have none of us staying to watch the ceremony, so don't press him." As Sey-Us stepped forward, Mai-Us took hold of his arm.

"We can come back tomorrow after they're done with their ceremony," Mai-Us said, hoping Sey-Us would heed him. Sey-Us squared his shoulders, spread his hands, and spoke in exaggerated conciliation.

"Dera, dera," he said, pointing to the landing party and himself.
The witch doctor was scrutinizing Sey-Us with open hostility, expressing distrust and displeasure at their presence. Sey-Us kept repeating the word, never letting the witch doctor lose eye contact with him, and pointing to himself and the landing party.

The chief hesitated. The witch doctor showed no equivocation as to the proper course of action for the chief. His impatience grew and he motioned to the warriors standing on the plaza and it looked as if he might incite them. The witch doctor shouted at the chief. The chief realized he had to act.

He spoke and the guards beside him and they raised their spears as the other warriors began moving forward.

Overcoming her fright, Ihand-A balanced herself against Risc-Um and rose on tiptoe to see what was happening. Her bronze fur caught the sun and the chief's eye at the same time. A shout caught in his throat and his mouth abruptly closed. The warriors and witch doctor froze at the sight of Ihand-A. They stared in a moment of stunned silence. The chief looked at the witch doctor seeking confirmation of what he was seeing and spoke swiftly. His arm went rigid and he pointed to Ihand-A

The witch doctor's angry tirade had been cut off at the chief's order. He stared in wonder at a suddenly very self-conscious Ihand-A. The warriors let their spears sag to the ground. It was unbelievable to Sey-Us. A blonde female was something they had never seen before.

"What's gotten into them, Mai-Us?" Sey-Us asked, bewildered.

"Exactly what I was afraid of," Mai-Us replied. "The chief said, behold the golden female of legend." Sey-Us wasn't aware the natives had seen Ihand-A and turned his eyes from the natives to Mai-Us.

"Meaning what?" Sey-Us asked, not understanding what the natives were talking about.

The chief now spoke with a voice full of ecstasy. The warriors intoned Gnok every time the chief spoke the name. He spoke with a shout and the warriors responded in servile tones. When he finished, the witch doctor seemed reassured, his eyes locked on Ihand-A in something akin to a religious trance. Mai-Us relayed the deal that had been offered them.

"The female of gold is Gnok's legacy from the ancient gods. You must sell us the golden female."

Now it was clear to Sey-Us what had happened and it was a development he didn't care for. He also noted the unease in Mai-Us' voice.

"Flaming hell! As if we don't have enough problems," Sey-Us
moaned, but turned an admiring eye to Ihand-A. The chief and witch doctor had lost their dislike and distrust and stepped closer to Mai-Us as the chief thrust out his arms in a regal gesture. Mai-Us didn't flinch and stood his ground. This would be the worst time to show fear especially since they had something very special, and the natives wanted her desperately. The chief spoke making gestures to the village and Ihand-A

"He wants to trade six of his females for Ihand-A," Mai-Us said, with no inflection in his voice. Ihand-A gasped but felt a little proud wishing she had been worth this much back in Icense.

"You got her into this, Sey-Us," Risc-Um said, sharply. "How are you going to get her out?" Risc-Um was annoyed that his advice hadn't been taken and now endangered them.

"It's going to take some fast talking to get us safely out of here, Sey-Us," Mai-Us said. He, too, was concerned for Ihand-A's safety as well as the rest of the party. The way the natives kept gaping at her made Mai-Us nervous. He also knew Sey-Us had an uncanny ability of extracting them from tight spots without casualties.

Sey-Us hadn't come all this way to fight with Gorillas and knew there was only one way to deal with them.

"Tell them she's our special magic, Mai-Us. We can't give her up without angering our gods. Let's hope they believe it." Sey-Us turned to look at Ihand-A.

"I never trade with savages, Ihand-A, it promotes cultural shock."

Mai-Us passed on Sey-Us' suggestion making the refusal as curtious as possible. The witch doctor flew into a rage, screaming and wagging a finger in the chief's face. Mai-Us translated.

"They refuse us Gnok's gift? They must give us the golden female or be made to pay for their refusal." Mai-Us turned a grim look to Sey-Us.

"I've heard enough," Risc-Um said. "I'm taking Ihand-A back to the ship."

"We better all get out of here before the witch doctor persuades the chief to block the path to the beach," Mai-Us said, in a firm tone.

"I agree," Sey-Us said, not about to disregard the advice. "Let's move away slowly. No sense in wearing out our welcome on the first visit." With confidence in their technological superiority over the natives, Sey-Us knew he had to back off in order to save lives. He fully understood that the party could easily overcome the natives as guns had the advantage over spears, but he hadn't come here for a confrontation. Sey-Us didn't want anyone to come to harm.

"Tell them we'll return tomorrow, Mai-Us. Then we can talk as friends." Mai-Us translated as a slow retirement began toward the beach.

At the edge of the village, they heard the chief shout and Sey-Us acted.

"Get moving," he ordered, stepping beside Ihand-A. "Do you realize the compliment the chief paid you? Six for one." Mai-Us looked over his shoulder and raised his hand.

"Tomorrow, friend." The retreat gathered speed with no lingering or undue rush. Half a dozen sailors, led by Risc-Um, moved ahead with Ihand-A in their midst. The rest followed, their rifles alert for anyone following them. Mai-Us followed them and true to form, Sey-Us brought up the rear.

As a parting sign of friendship, Sey-Us tossed the natives a casual wave before vanishing around the hut. The stunned natives stared in disbelief as Sey-Us jauntily slid out of sight. The party hurried along the dirt path, still unoccupied, for which the landing party breathed a sigh of relief.

They came to the head of the peninsula and hurried toward the boats. They had become a single file, stretching like a snake, with everyone glancing over their shoulder for signs of pursuit that didn't materialize. The idea that the natives were just letting them walk away was disturbing to Mai-Us. Like everything else about these natives, it was completely out of character for any island tribe on the eve of a big religious ceremony. Thespa stepped beside Mai-Us as they walked on.

"There were natives in the huts, Captain," Thespa said. "I heard a little one make a noise and what a smack he got." He shifted the case to his other shoulder.

Risc-Um released the hand he had been holding so protectively with a visible show of relief.

"I can't believe it," Risc-Um said, looking back the way they had come. "They're not following and that's welcome news." Sey-Us and Mai-Us were coming at a quick pace as they realized they had gotten too far behind for safety. The sailors stood around Risc-Um and Ihand-A as she glanced at them

"I'm not hostile to anyone," she said. "Just the same, if there had been a fight, I would have been glad not to have missed it." They all knew she was half laughing but scared. They also knew she meant
what she had said.

Ihand-A had a slightly prideful look as she began to finger her fur that of late had become so greatly prized.

Risc-Um glanced at her with displeasure but grudgingly had to admire her spirit. She had proven she had no lack of courage and the crew would now accept her as one of them. She felt a deeper sense of friendship with these sailors than she had ever felt toward her former University friends. She felt even closer to Risc-Um.

"You certainly have pluck, Ihand-A," Mai-Us said. "If that had been another female she would have made for the beach."

"And for that, you must be rewarded," Sey-Us said, in a respectful tone. "From now on you're my personal aide." Mai-Us cut a slice of fruit and motioned everyone into the boats. He climbed in beside Sey-Us who gave him a puzzled look.

"I don't care for this turn of events, Sey-Us. They should have tried to take her or come after us," Mai-Us said, shaking his head. "It's too out of character for natives to behave like this, especially when they want Ihand-A so badly." Sey-Us felt the same way but decided to put a good face on their escape.

"Relax, Mai-Us,. They can't do a thing once we're back on the No'mo." Mai-Us gave him a sharp look.

"I'm not so sure. We better keep a tight watch onboard tonight."

"Tomorrow we'll break out some trinkets as gifts for the chief and witch doctor," Sey-Us said. "That should make our position better and mellow them a bit." The boats had to be pushed through the shallows before the oars could be used. The sailors jumped in and began rowing. Slowly, the No'mo drew near offering them safety. Mai-Us had a growing uneasiness that he decided to give no voice to at present.

FALSE SECURITY

The moment of their departure from the beach, the mood changed to one of good spirits at the outcome of their first encounter with the natives of Scumm Island. But as they began to weigh the peril they had dared, it dampened their mood to one of glum acceptance that worse might yet come. By the time they arrived at the ship, all were quiet, lost in their own thoughts. Relief filled them as they climbed onboard. Only one question – the foreboding enigma – prompted Sey-Us to have only one idea in mind. Gnok! What was it? How did it fit into the native religion? Was it exclusive to Scumm Island?

After Mai-Us, Risc-Um, and Ihand-A assembled in the chart room, Sey-Us bluntly stated what was on his mind as well as theirs.

"I want to find out what this Gnok is. What made the natives think Ihand-A was a gift to it from ancient gods? The golden female of legend. Gnok's heavenly gift. I'm determined to solve the mystery."

"Could Gnok be a higher chief?" Ihand-A asked.

"Not a chance," Mai-Us replied, gravely. "You may not have seen that Gnok's bride had been drugged. They wouldn't have had to do that if she was being fixed up with a big chief." Mai-Us paused and cut a slice of fruit.

"But drugged she was," Mai-Us continued. "She just sat there and paid no attention to what was going on."

"Mai-Us is right," Sey-Us said. "She would have been glad to be the wife of a chief. I can see only one reason to drug her – to keep her calm."

"Nothing we saw on that island made sense," Risc-Um said. "That female was drugged while we watched, and I think it was the flowers she wore." Sey-Us nodded.

"I found myself feeling odd when I stood by a bush with same sort of flowers," Sey-Us said.

"She has my sympathy," Ihand-A said.

"I'm certain those natives who were imitating primaloids are the solution," Sey-Us said. "But I haven't figured out how." He was still reflecting over what he had seen and kept trying to fit the pieces into
the puzzle.

"What makes you think that?" Risc-Um asked. He had been forming his own opinion about the grusome dancers and it wasn't pleasant to consider.

"I believe they were acting in place of the real spouse," Sey-Us explained. "There was a huge gong above the gate and I saw a native ready to strike it when the witch doctor saw us and stopped the show. I think the gong was going to be struck and the female taken outside the gate."

"If I understand you correctly," Risc-Um said. "It's no wonder they were so hopping mad." Ihand-A got an annoyed look.

"Well I don't understand," she said, bluntly. "I'm not stupid just slow to understand the motives of savages." Risc-Um and Sey-Us exchanged glances. Sey-Us looked at her.

"The witch doctor was about to have her taken out," Sey-Us said.
"Now what do you suppose was waiting for her on the other side?"
Risc-Um took up the explanation.

"It has to be something that would have frightened her so bedly she had to be drugged. And make no mistake, the rest of that tribe is also fearful of whatever it is." Risc-Um saw she still didn't understand.

"Sey-Us and I figure it this way," Risc-Um continued, finding it difficult to explain what was unknown. "The village is on the peninsula side of the wall – safe.

Beyond the wall there's nothing but jungle and the menace that keeps the tribe to preserve the wall. The female was to be sacrificed to whatever lives in the jungle."

"The witch doctor was about to send the female out," Sey-Us carried on. "The native by the gong was going to signal Gnok to come for his bride. Do you understand now, Ihand-A?" She understood and it made her feel sick.

"It can also be assumed that female isn't the first bride," Mai-Us injected, in a solemn tone.

"You can't mean – No!" Ihand-A was very uneasy.

"You have to accept it," Sey-Us said. "That female wasn't the first living sacrifice to Gnok." He hoped he conveyed the sense of danger that their encounter with the natives meant to her.

"Most likely, sacrifices are regular rituals," Mai-Us said. "Like before the rainy season or on what they consider a special day."

"We've seen sacrifices on other islands," Risc-Um said. "They
were to placate wild animals, blood sacrifices. But here is something
different here." Risc-Um grew uneasier as they spoke.

"I'm beginning to form a picture of Gnok," Sey-Us said, a twinkle coming to his eyes. "That wall wasn't built to keep ordinary jungle beasts out. There were nine proxies dancing, I believe, because that was the only way the natives could match the size of Gnok. Those primaloid masks had no model for them."

"If he's as big as you estimate," Mai-Us said. "It would make the natives like toys." Risc-Um nodded.

"It would also account for the size of that gate and wall," Risc-Um added.

"There can't be such a beast," Ihand-A said, emphatically.

"At least, none that have survived from the primal stage of Ephus." Sey-Us looked at her with enlightenment.

"You may just have hit on the truth, Ihand-A," Sey-Us said, excited. Risc-Um looked at Sey-Us amazed.

"You don't believe that, do you?" Risc-Um asked, a strong surge
of adventure rushing through him. Mai-Us shook his head considering such an idea nonsense.

"Let's not discard the idea because it seems impossible," Sey-Us said. "Any idea about Scumm Island needs to be fully explored." Eleation was growing in Sey-Us at the thought of such a momentous discovery. And only he could have found it. He continued his argument with a sense of elan.

"This island is remote and those ruins are ancient. It could possibly be the dwelling place of a primal beast. One could have threatened those who built that wall for protection. The size of the wall is all the evidence we have until we get on the other side of it." Sey-Us couldn't hide his elation.

"If we can capture it – take it back alive – we will never have to go on another boring expedition. We would be set for life." Risc-Um laughed.

"I've never been on a boring expedition with you, Sey-Us," Risc-Um said, with a tone of irony. "This is my third and I still wonder how my hide is hanging on my bones in one piece." Sey-Us' suggestion filled him with excitement, but he saw the obstruction of getting through that gate.

"The natives will prevent us from getting through the gate," Risc-Um said. "How do you intend getting past them without trouble?" The thoughts racing through Risc-Um's mind excited him like no others, but reality intruded.

"Where does Ihand-A fit into this picture?" Risc-Um asked. Sey-Us showed annoyance, contemplated the question, then chuckled.

"Will you let me run my own show, Risc-Um? I know you yield to emotions, and Ihand-A's a grand choice. But don't expect me to pass up the possibility of a lifetime. Think what it will mean if our assumption about the island is correct." Sey-Us paused, tugged on his ear, and continued.

"I don't know how any of us might be affected. This is going to take careful planning and a lot of luck."

"It's going to take more than a lot of luck," Mai-Us said. Sey-Us glanced at him knowing he was right but hoping it might prove easier than expected.

"I'll work out how we proceed," Sey-Us said. "We'll discuss it at dinner." Risc-Um got a cynical look not recalling anytime Sey-Us had ever discussed how something should work.

"In the meantime, Risc-Um, post a watch," Sey-Us said. "And
stress they must remain alert, especially after dark."

"I've got a feeling that witch doctor is up to no good," Mai-Us said. "Now that those drums have started again there's no telling what they might try."

"I'll post the watch and check with them regularly, Skipper," Risc-Um said, with a sense of foreboding.

The drums gradually revived into a more exultant, savage thunder. Moreso than before the No'mo party had landed. Eventually they became a low drone making the beat seem a background for primitive minds to think.

After posting the watch, Risc-Um returned to the bridge and stood staring sullenly at the island.

It would soon be dark and for the first time Risc-Um was dreading the coming night. The drums were a constant reminder of danger.

"It's going to be a long night, Skipper," Risc-Um predicted, dourly. "And those drums aren't going to ease anyone's nerves." Mai-Us regarded his back and shook his head.

"A dark night isn't so bad when you consider we're too far off shore for them to try a surprise raid without being seen," Mai-Us said. "Sey-Us is certainly right about how you feel about Ihand-A." But Mai-Us, too, was tense about the coming night.

"I just don't like the sound of those drums, Skipper. They give me the creeps."

Into the evening the drums persisted, troubling Risc-Um. They sat
down to dinner as the tropic twilight was deepening into darkness. Risc-Um couldn't explain his growing dread and tried not to show it. Sey-Us kept up a trivial monologue through dinner. Pushing his plate away, Sey-Us seemed ready for business.

"There are too many variables to form a solid plan," Sey-Us said. "However, early tomorrow we'll go ashore with a small armed party."

"I wouldn't count on force to deter the natives, Sey-Us," Mai-Us said.

"I'm counting on their never having heard gunfire," Sey-Us said. "That should scare them into hiding for awhile."

"Then what?" Risc-Um asked. Sey-Us picked up his glass of grape juice and regarded Risc-Um with a confident look.

"Then we go after Gnok," he replied, lifting his glass in toast. He felt he was about to conquer the unknown again.

Risc-Um pushed his glass aside and turned his eyes to Ihand-A It was a deliberate gesture Sey-Us couldn't misinterpret.

"Ihand-A will remain on the ship," Sey-Us said, watching Risc-Um's reaction.

"I'm glad to hear that," Mai-Us said. Ihand-A gave each a disgusted look and turned her attention to Sey-Us.

"I'm willing to return to the island," she said, glancing at Risc-Um with an annoyed look.

"I usually don't like going without my aide," Sey-Us said. "Under normal circumstances there are perils that can be measured and prepared for. Here we have unknown perils that make it difficult to know what measures to take." He paused for a drink of juice.

"This will be a preliminary reconnoitering," he continued. "If things go well, Ihand-A, you can come ashore later." Risc-Um could now think of things other than her safety.

"Why don't I lead the landing party?" Risc-Um asked, his tone betraying his eagerness. "We'll convince the natives we mean business." Sey-Us regarded him with an irritated look.

"That's why I'm going," Sey-Us said, firmly. "I want to avoid trouble, if possible." Risc-Um wasn't yet ready to give up.

"Suppose by some mischance you were to be incapacitated, Sey-Us? The expedition would be held up, maybe even abandoned. But if I fell over a rock it wouldn't matter."

"What makes you think you're expendable?" Ihand-A asked, with a look that made Risc-Um's blood run cold. He just grinned not wanting to antagonize her. Sey-Us smacked his hand on the table to
get their attention.

"Hold it, both of you. Risc-Um's ready to give his all, as usual, now I've decided to leave you in safety. And you, Ihand-A, are ready to crown him because he feels adventuresome. My point is, when I organize an expedition I lead it. I'll not make an exception now." Sey-Us checkled.

"I take back what I said about you going soft, Risc-Um. It's apparent you're soft only in your heart." Risc-Um couldn't hide the flush of embarrassment and was glad only three friends were there to see.

"I've got to check with the watch," Risc-Um said, stood, and hurried out the hatch as Mai-Us and Sey-Us had a good laugh. Ihand-A regarded them with an indignant look.

"I'm not impressed by such conduct, Dr. Sey-Us," she said, rising with a noble elegance. At the hatch, she looked back with a sly smile before stepping into the darkness of the deck.

The drums rumbled and seemed to cast a spell of waiting across the water. Each throb seemed a physical impact to Ihand-A as she stepped on deck. She felt the drums were anticipating something and shuddered. She saw armed sailors making their rounds, meeting at intervals, and returning to their movement.

Other sailors were out too seeking relief from the stifling heat below. Now that the sun had set, a dead heat seemed to have taken over. Pablae was one of those seeking elusive coolness. He sprawled on a hatch cover in his frayed pants hoping for some small comfort.

"Good evening, Pablae," Ihand-A said, coming down from the bridge. He sat up and turned to face her.

"Evening, Ihand-A. I heard the chief made a grand offer for you. How did you feel about it?" She sat down on the hatch cover and clasped her hands on her lap.

"It was exciting. But after Dr. Sey-Us and Risc-Um explained what it meant, it really frightened me."

After the short exchange they sat in silence. Ihand-A took in the view of the stars in the black vault of the sky.

Sey-Us and Mai-Us stepped out to the railing and listened.

"I wish those confounded drums would cease," Mai-Us said. Sey-Us felt the same but had something else in mind.

"If I thought I could learn something I would sneak back in a minute," Sey-Us said, feeling impatient. Once he had made his decision he was eager to implement it. Waiting was frustrating for

him. He didn't notice the disbelieving look Mai-Us had turned to him.

"You're better off here than sneaking around that island," Mai-Us said, solemnly. "No telling what those natives would do if they caught you. Especially after the way we snubbed them." Sey-Us glanced at him.

"I know, Skipper. But I hate missing any part of what we saw today. That's why I've got to learn the mysteries of the island."

"I wouldn't mind if we sailed right now," Mai-Us said. "It's those natives, Sey-Us! I've got an awful feeling about that island, an evil feeling."

"Faming hell! Don't tell me you're getting the jitters." Mai-Us rubbed the corner of his eye.

"I've had a bad feeling about that island since I laid eyes on it. And you know my instinct has been right most of the time." Mai-Us wasn't certain he was trying to convince Sey-Us or himself. The unease he felt was greater than he had ever experienced before. This was a situation the like of which Sey-Us had never gotten them into before. Everything about the island was unknown and that made it more unsettling.

"I think I'll stay here and make certain everything remains quiet, Sey-Us. I've got to work on the log."

They stared at the glowing fires lighting up the island. Sey-Us pointed to the largest.

"Look at that fire, Skipper. The natives are getting ready to appease their god, too preoccupied to bother with us."

"So it seems. But appearances can be deceptive."

"I'll stay here with you. I couldn't sleep anyway. I'll mark this island's position on the main chart."

Pablae glanced at Ihand-A whose face showed clearly in the circle of light falling from the porthole above her head. It had cooled very little with the coming of darkness and the humidity made it more uncomfortable. There hadn't been a decent breeze since late afternoon; the wind abating after dark which wasn't unusual in the tropics. They saw distant flashes of lightning on the horizon, but it was too far away to offer any chance for a cooling rain.

"Want to talk about what happened today, Ihand-A?" She glanced at him and slightly shrugged.

"I'm not certain I understand what happened. I feel sorry for the female native who is to be sacrificed."

"Female you say?" She nodded.

"Yes. That's when the fuss about me began. They wanted to give
Dr. Sey-Us six of their females for me. Because of my bright fur, they thought I would make a better sacrifice." She suddenly recalled the clutch of fear she had experienced when she realized the natives wanted her.

"It seems I've walked into an ancient legend. A legend and me! It sounds so silly, but the natives were quite serious."

"I did hear something about you being called a special bride for Gnok," Pablae said.

"The bride of Gnok," Ihand-A said, and shuddered. "Pablae, do you think Gnok is real or just some native superstition?" Pablae patted her hand.

104

"It's probably superstition. Every tribe on an island has a similar story. Usually it's an odd shaped tree or boulder that holds a spirit. But it's always something they can identify." He paused and thought.

"I'll bet the female is hidden. That witch doctor could most likely tell you where they went."

"You think that's all there is to it?" Ihand-A asked, feeling somewhat better. She saw him nod.

"Witch doctors have been known to have private harems miles from the village. They might fool the tribe but they're not fooling this old sailor." Ihand-A laughed and stretched feeling more at ease.

Risc-Um stepped through a hatch and came toward them using a flashlight. He stopped and glanced at Ihand-A.

"I need help below, Pablae."

"Right, Mr. Risc-Um." He got to his feet and headed toward the hatch. Ihand-A saw Risc-Um was now composed.

"Hadn't you better get some sleep?" he asked. "You've had quite a day for a novice explorer."

"I am rather tired," Ihand-A said. "But I want to sit here for awhile." Risc-Um nodded, patted her shoulder, and headed toward the nearest sailor making his round, spoke with him, and went through the hatch he had appeared through.

She stretched and felt sleepy since her talk with Pablae had relieved her tension. She could forget about Gnok. She stood and walked to where the deck narrowed into a lane leading past the lower part of the superstructure. For an instant, she paused and looked around, apprehensive. The glow from a porthole flared on her before she moved into shadow. She started when the drums soared in volume and fell to a clucking tattoo.

On the bridge, Sey-Us was reassuring Mai-Us of the success of the expedition.

"I tell you, Mai-Us, we'll make playmates of them. They were upset because of our interrupting their ceremony. I'm confident we can convince them it was a harmless mistakes and that we want to be friends."

"I'm not sure we can trust those savage devils," Mai-Us said, in a warning tone. "You recall them saying we had spoiled their magic? And the threat that we would have to pay for not trading Ihand-A? That meant they would have to find a new bride and it doesn't make me feel easier as to where she might be found." Mai-Us gazed at the island.

"You don't understand, Sey-Us. They weren't angry with us, they were furious." Sey-Us was thinking of something else.

"Wouldn't it be great if they have to do it over, Skipper? Only this time, I could be there to see the whole show." Mai-Us regarded his boss with an incredulous expression and shook his head.

"Uou're incorrigible, Sey-Us. How do others put up with you? Especially your collaegues at the University."

Risc-Um came on the bridge wiping his forehead with a cloth.

"I've checked with the watch, Skipper. Everything's quiet. Has Ihand-A been up here?"

"Isn't she still on deck?" Mai-Us asked.

"Been over half an hour since you seen here, eh," Sey-Us said, with a devilish grin. Risc-Um turned an irate look to him.

"You know, Sey-Us, I'm glad I never went to the University. It seems education makes some people pompus." Risc-Um turned, stepped back through the hatch, and headed for where he had last seen her.

He found Pablae looking around. Except for the water lapping softly against the ship's sides the No'mo was quiet. Risc-Um looked to Pablae.

"You seen Ihand-A?"

"Not since I went below, Mr. Risc-Um." Risc-Um decided to check her cabin as uneasiness grew in him.

"Maybe she turned in," Pablae suggested. He left Pablae looking into the darkness. Disappointed, Pablae turned away and started alone the lane Ihand-A had earlier traveled. As he stepped into the darkness, his foot struck something that went clattering along the deck. He bent down, picked it up, and moved into the light of a porthole. At first, he couldn't identify it, and then his blood ran cold.

"To the deck," Pablae shouted, running back to the main deck. "To the deck. Everybody to the deck now." The men on watch were first to respond, appearing from all directions. Others came running too.

Risc-Um heard Pablae's call and came out of Ihand-A's cabin and almost collided with Mai-Us and Sey-Us coming from the bridge. They pushed through the sailors to an agitated Pablae. Risc-Um didn't notice what Pablae held out to them until he turned the flashlight on it.

"Look at this, Captain. I just found it by the lower deck house," Pablae said, rapidly.

"Flaming hell! A native bracelet," Sey-Us said, taking it from Pablae. Simultaneously, they realized natives had been able to come aboard without being seen by the watch.

"Those savages were here, sir?" A sailor asked.

"I don't see how," another replied.

"Search the ship," Sey-Us ordered.

"Where's Ihand-A?" Risc-Um asked. Mai-Us and Sey-Us exchanged alarmed glances as they understood what her absence could mean.

"In her cabin," Sey-Us said. Risc-Um shook his head.

"I just checked." The voices of the sailors came along the port side toward them. It seemed impossible that natives could have gotten aboard without one of the watch seeing them.

"Did any of you hear anything?" Mai-Us asked.

"Not a thing, Captain," a sailor replied. The otheres nodded.

"This is what Pablae found," Risc-Um said, holding up the bracelet.

"Portside lower deck house," Pablae added. Risc-Um looked to Sey-Us and Mai-Us.

"Makes sense," risc-Um said, to himself.

"What makes sense?" Mai-Us asked.

"No natives were onboard, Skipper," Risc-Um replied. "That's why they weren't seen. Ihand-A would have had to pass the lower deck house to get to her cabin. They came along side, tossed a line over the rail and climbed the side of the ship. They must have seen me talking with her. When she went to her cabin, they grabbed her."

"How could they have known she would come that way?" Pablae asked.

"Blind luck," Risc-Um replied. "They got her just at the time when all the watch was out of sight." Mai-Us' voice thundered through the darkness.

"Bosun, prepare the boats to get underway. Give everyone a rifle and generous portion of ammunition."

The glow of flashlights and bustline feet carried across the deck. The bosun's whistle sounded in the night, the grate and click of davits, the metallic clang as bullets fell from eager hands to the deck, all expressed the pressure of a crisis. As they regarded Risc-Um in the light from a porthole, none noticed the increase in brightness of the fires on the island as they seemed to light up the sky.

Sey-Us came to Mai-Us who was directing the boat crews and saw they were loading vapor bombs as well as other provisions.

"Skipper, you don't think they would…" Sey-Us didn't finish as the idea seemed too fantastic, and too good to be true. It was the excuse he needed to get past that wall.

"We have no way of knowing, Sey-Us," Mai-Us replied. "But you
saw how badly they wanted her. It seems they went to a lot of trouble
to get her."

"We can't waste time, Skipper." Mai-Us nodded.

"Set up a watch to remain onboard, Risc-Um," Mai-Us said. "And form a search party as soon as we land." The last of the searching sailors had returned and reported no trace of Ihand-A.

GNOK'S PRIZE

Eager native hands pressed Ihand-A to the bottom of the silently moving praho. Another hand covered her mouth as she struggled futilely. She had not had a chance to utter a sound since her moment of seizure. Hot smelly hands trussed and muzzled her in the first seconds of struggle. She had been able to jerk a bracelet off one of her captors. The feeling of apprehension should have been warning enough as she started along the dark deck. Her mouth, arms, and legs had been deftly and quickly snared. Once secured, she had been conveyed from one set of hands to another down from the ship. As one hand was removed from her mouth another replaced it. Ihand-A was terrified. No fiction she had ever read could express the trepidation that swept her in waves and made her feel her body was covered with unspeakable things. It went beyond the dark corner of childhood fear, surpassing the dread of an unwakable nightmare. Her only thought was to cry out for help, call for risc-Um. But she suspected that if the smelly hand were lifted from her mouth the fear that constricted her throat wouldn't give forth her voice. Her legs, let loose, refused to move.

After the praho grated onto the beach, her abductors dragged her to her feet on land, but she couldn't stand alone. Ihand-A fell face down on the sand that was giving off a light phosphorescence. They jerked her roughly to her feet, forced her mouth open, and poured in a foul tasting liquid from a wooden cup.

The witch doctor wasted no time in ordering a thickset shadow to hoist her over his shoulder and hurry off through the darkness. Several times her carrier was changed, always after given a growling order.

The third time Ihand-A heard it, her heart skipped a beat as realized the order was from the chief. She hadn't been aware of his presence with the raiding party.

She began to feel very odd and realized the drink had been some drug that was now affecting her. She was carried through the village, past large bright fires, and placed on the altar before the gate. The top of the wall was aglow with natives brandishing torches. To Ihand-A, the area now seemed to be in three colors; yellow, orange, and black.

The tribe massed around her and above her just as they had for the young female. Lines of natives filed past on either side of the now draped bride. The chief had taken the same remote stance and was clad in the gaudiness of feathers. Ihand-A noted all this with exceptional clarity but no independent thought came to mind. The witch doctor positioned her last carriers to her sides, but she had no thought of going anywhere. He then took his proper position for the ceremony.

The drug had now affected her to where she not only couldn't think but she couldn't move. The carved steps leading to the altar was vacant but she saw no significance in that. Nearby, standing alone, a doleful face regarded her without emotion. Ihand-A dimly recognized her as the flower garlanded femals who had been the earlier bride and now was dressed as the other females. This fact failed to give Ihand-A any clue as to what was happening to her. Her mind couldn't corrolate sight and fact.

At a signal from the witch doctor, she was lifted and transported to a higher stage of the altar where more flowers were draped over her. She sat stiffly seeing everything but it remained incomprehensible to her. It was a stupor induced by the drug and flowers. Nervous activity throbbed behind her and she was moved closer to the gate.

The witch doctor was avid to set the ritual in motion. Too much time had been consumed in repeating the ceremony for the new bride, and he kept prodding others to hurry.

Ihand-A had a vague picture in her mind that so much bustle had to be caused by the belief that her rescuers would be coming soon, but It aroused no hope in her. She felt she had been withouthope from her first muffled cry. She had the resolute conviction that the great mystery of the island had entrapped her, that rescue was a forlorn hope that couldn't become a reality.

The natives began a loud chant as their ranks swayed in the firelight to a hypnotic tempo. The witch doctor performed his quaint dance until he stood beside Ihand-A Once more, the primaloid imitators sprung from the chanting mass and the chief came into the ceremony. He stepped forward and his arm shot into the air. Ten warriors rushed to the huge log holding the gate shut, split into two groups, one at each end of the log. One group began pushing and the other pulling. Ihand-A knew the chief had ordered the gate opened. Others began tugging the gate open as the chief shouted and the warrior at the apex of the gate struck a robust blow on the massive gong.

Briefly aroused by the booming resonance, Ihand-A recalled the signal Risc-Um had spoken of. A signal telling Gnok his new bride waited. She was to be sacrificed to – what? Still it meant nothing to her paralyzed mind. At the gourth strike on the gong, all chanting ceased. Ihand-A didn't feel a paret of what was occurring. She was here as an observer for Sey-Us. The ranks at the sides of the gate headed for the top of the wall to welcome the arrival of their god. Cries of joy mixed with anxiety spilled from the natives along the top of the wall. As the steps became congested, others began climbing rickety branch ladders and vines to the top.

112

On top of the wall, they began their chant again, swaying to the movement of the flames of the torches they held. As expectation built, the torches were thrust beyond the wall illuminating the base on the far side of the gate. In the distance came the sound of a mighty beast and the natives broke into wild cheering. The chief quickly stabbed a finger at Ihand-A and shouted. The gatekeepers struggled to get the gate open wider and stood staring fearful into the darkness. They were determined that what was coming wouldn't be given any chance to come through the gate. If Gnok should become angered by something, it could prove terrible for the natives. The chief shouted another command and the gong was struck spreading resonance across the dark jungle.

Atop the wall, natives who had torches exctended them out as far as they could. Beyond the gate, the torchlight dimly illuminated a weed-infested field whose edges faded into the green-black shadows of the jungle. An ancient stone stage with two grandly carved pillars rose from the green carpet below it. Two natives hustled Ihand-A through the gate and up on the stage where they stretched her arms to the pillars. The chief shouted an anxious order as her wrists were slipped through vines and drawn tight. They huried down the steps, as she stood on wobbly, weak legs. She bsrely understood her predicament as she looked around with bleary eyes.

Another loud shout from the chief and the gong sounded again. The vibrations seemed to stun Ihand-A. The natives began swaying and chanting deliriously. The wedding garb she wore fell from her and curled around her feet. Her guards rushed through the gate and helped push it shut with a thud. Ihand-A was alone outside the ancient monolithic wall, a prisoner in its dark shadow.

From the direction of the mountain came a deep, unreal sound that met the voices of the natives. The sound came eerily through the darkness to Ihand-A She knew it was an animal, a large animal, yet she wasn't frightened.

"Gnok! Gnok! Gnok!" he netives roared as they jumped up and down. The torchbearers erupted into a wild jubilant cry that seemed deafening to Ihand-A

"Gnok! Gnok! Gnok!" It had became a chant without losing any volume.

A sense of menace lifted Ihand-A's eyes and she looked around. She saw her wrists and knew what was causing her pain. She began to struggle against the bite of of the vines. Looking over her shoulder, her mind cleared as she watched the natives on top of the wall. Turning back, she became aware of a darker shadow from which arose an immense roar. The shape pulled her vision into sharp focus and she stood frozen. The shadow seemed to detatch itself from the darkness and stepped into the torchlight becoming a nightmare reality.

Ihand-A watched Gnok move into the glow and look at the top of the wall. Pouring out s defiant roar, she saw its mouth filled with yellow stained teeth. White hands drummed against a hairy barrel chest in challenge. It had hair on top of its head and along its arms and hands. It looked at her through deep blue eyes that seemed to paralyze her. Looking back to the wall, it hesitated, then seemed to understand the shouts and gestures.

The drug began to lose its effect and Ihand-A became aware of her quandary. The beast stepped to the stage and bellowed at the captive who was alone, helpless, and filled with fear. The natives became suddenly still and the air felt heavy, without a breath of wind to stir the trees. Ihand-A" scream of desperation echoed away into the stillness. Gnok stepped back, turned his head from side to side, and

114

watched her. He emitted a horrendous growl and smashed his fist into a tree that shattered it into splinters. A roar sped across the jungle letting it know he was master.

He lifted his hand from the shattered tree and was about to touch this unusual golden female that struggled against her bonds. He withdrew his hand and turned his eyes back to the wall. No sound came from the natives, only Ihand-A whimpering as she struggled to free herself. He turned back to his cautious investigation. He found he couldn't pick her up and quickly saw why. The vines offered no obstacle to him as they snapped easily in his fingers.

He lifted her close to his face and took a long look at the strange female who had just went limp in his hand, sagging over his thumb. Her fur and clothing were a mystery to him. In distraction, he began a low rumble as he turned her over in the manner of a half grown Orang might inspect an unconscious bird.

Looking at the natives, he emitted a subdued growl. The natives were shouting joyfully when strange voices and sounds joined the clamor. Gnok paid no heed as he gently placed Ihand-A in the crook of an arm, turned his back on the wall, and started away. The heavy, urgent moan of the opening gate drew no attention from him. An accusing figure leaped through the gate, cried out, and fired a hissing something past Gnok's' ear. He only vaulted away with a lively step taking him into the safety of the jungle.

PURSUIT

Sey-Us ordered the rowers forward, making the boat glide swiftly through the water. After landing, Sey-Us deployed the sailors for the taxing run up the beach to the village. The moment the gate was opened, Risc-Um took command and coordinated the pursuit of Gnok. Risc-Um alone had gotten a good look at the beast before it disappeared into the jungle. He had seen Ihand-A cradled like a doll in its arm. The shot that had quickened Gnok's step had been fired by Risc-Um.

"I'll take over the chase." Sey-Us nodded.

"Very well, Risc-Um, but I'm going too." Sey-Us' tone left no room for argument and Risc-Um knew Sey-Us wasn't about to be miss such a chance. Risc-Um turned to the sailors.

"I need ten volunteers," Risc-Um barked.

"I'll go," Pablae said, as a chorus of voices joined him. Everyone had volunteered, making Risc-Um select the more familiar sailors. Pablae kept iunsisting until Risc-Um became annoyed.

"You keep watch here, Pablae. If anything happened to you, Ihand-A would have my hide nailed to her cabin door."

"You still have the vapor bombs, Thespa?" Sey-Us asked, loudly. "We're going to need them in the jungle."

"Right here, Doctor," Thespa said, stepping beside Sey-Us. He was excited and trying to control it. A larger sailor offered to take the bombs but Thespa hefted them onto his shoulder.

"No way," Thespa said. "I carried them before and I'm carrying
them now." Sey-Us turned to Risc-Um.

"I'll have the skipper remain here," Sey-Us said. "And make certain the gate remains open."

"That suits me," Risc-Um said. "Let's just get moving."

Risc-Um made a quick check to be sure every sailor had extra ammunition and a flashlight. Sey-Us checked the case counting the vapor bombs.

"We'll travel in single file," Risc-Um said. "Don't lose sight of the person in front of you."

"I want to emphasize that," Sey-Us said. "If anyone gets lost out ther, you'll never be found. So stay close to your shipmates." He was impatient to be loosed on the hunt.

"Let's move out," Risc-Um ordered, striding toward the gate.

They set off trotting, Sey-Us beside Risc-Um at the front of the column. They halted by the stage and Sey-Us gave it a quick measurement and looked to Risc-Um with an incredulous expression. It was hard to comprehand the size of the beast.

"What did it look like risc-Um?"

"There wasn't much light," Risc-Um replied, having a hard time believing the size of the beast. "But its chest was taller than these pillars by a good ten feet, and that was when it was bending down." Sey-Us' eyes widened.

"Those pillars are at least twenty-five feet! Are you certain, Risc-Um?" He nodded with a grim look.

"We've got to get a move on if we want to catch up with it."

Moving through the jungle, they heard running water and came to a ravine that should guide them through the tableland toward the mountain.

"We'll follow this," Sey-Us said. "It's possible the beast also came this way." Risc-Um nodded and they moved forward using flashlights to mark out their path. The lights were only effective for four or five feet in the dense jungle. The ravine widened into a moderate, gushing stream that flowed from the mountain toward the sea. The ravine had narrowed channeling the water into a swift current. Sey-Us pointed to it.

"A good swimmer like you, Risc-Um, should be able to come along this natural chute," Sey-Us said. "It would be much faster than a jungle trail." Risc-Um noted that Sey-Us was panting from the pace they had been moving.

"We've got to find the beast's trail," Risc-Um said. He had just
finished when one of the sailors cried out and was quickly joined by the others.

"Here's a track, Mr. Risc-Um," a sailor said, getting to his feet inside it. They stared at the large, deep track and the direction it was heading. Risc-Um made certain the sailor who had fallen was all right.

"We're headed in the right direction," Risc-Um said, confidently. "Let's move on."

Moving through the jungle became a slow, brutal ordeal marked by bruised shins and awkward stumbles. One sailor slipped and fell into the stream and was washed a way down before grasping a juttling root. As his shipmates reached him, he was clinging tenaciously against the current and maneuvering to keep away from a sliver of rock knifing from the bank.

"I held onto my rifle," he proclaimed, proudly, when he was hauled back on solid ground. He had had a good soaking but wasn't hurt. They returned to the trail.

When they came to the top of a rise, they emerged into less dense jungle. Here huge trees stood with trunks covered in a lush tangle of vines. The stream widened here and moved into higher sountry along a gradual slope. It was still jungle and that meant slow going through a darkness the like of which none had ever experienced.

"This plateau slopes toward the mountain," Sey-Us said. "That must be where he's heading." Here the ground was too solid for tracks, and that baffled them. It was imperative they find a track if they were to continue following Gnok.

"Everybody look around," Risc-Um ordered. He felt unnerved at the thought of losing the trail.

"Here's a crushed bush, Mr. Risc-Um," Thespa said. "Something big came this way and not long ago." They discovered other broken branches and crushed shrubs.

"Here's a track," a sailor said. It was clear and not far past the crushed brush indicating Gnok was following the stream toward that mountain. That was all Risc-Um needed to know. He took the lead, but the thick undergrowth slowed their pace. They moved on with only one direction in mind.

An odd sound began to penetrate the depths of the jungle.

"Birds! Hundreds of them," Sey-Us said, in a jungle with a growing volume of sound. It was waking up and telling them it was dawn.

"We'll have full daylight soon," Sey-Us said. "That will make
tracking easier." A dim hope for Ihand-A's rescue began to encourage him.

"And we can step up the pace," Risc-Um added. "Maybe gain some ground on the beast." They moved for some time without any apparent change in the light. Gradually they began to see shadows as light pierced the canopy of trees. They paused in a shaft of sunlight whose glow was on another huge print. Only then did the full impact of Gnok's size leap into their consciousness.

"Look at the size of that!" Thespa exclaimed, setting his load on the ground. The others stared in awe.

"He's bigger than any living thing I've ever seen," one sailor commented.

"At least he's still heading in the same direction," Sey-Us said. Risc-Um glanced at the sailors.

"We can't afford to be surprised," Risc-Um warned. "Stay alert and keep your rifles ready."

"You needn't remind us, Mr. Risc-Um," Thespa said, pushing the safety to the off position.

Later, an ample clearing revealed itself. Scathed by trees they couldn't avoid in darkness, welted by branches that had stung them, they stumbled into it wore out. It was full light and except for a thin drifting mist amid the foliage, everything was visible. They came on another of the great tracks but it no longer had the power to impress them as they sank to the ground for a short rest. After afew minutes rest, Risc-Um stood.

"Let's move on." As he started, a warning came from Sey-Us.

"Wait. Look there." Risc-Um stopped, turned, and looked in the direction of Sey-Us' extended arm. The sailors erupted in panicky cries as they saw the beast.

"Gnok," one shouted. It wasn't, as Risc-Um knew, but it was an immense beast emerging from the jungle. It was covered with light gray scales and had a small head on a long swaying neck. It came forward in an awkward skittering movement on four thick legs. Its forelegs were low toward the base of the neck and covered with thick skin.

As the sailors took cover, Sey-Us had his first inclination of the island's mysteries. His first sight of the beast had filled him with fear.

"Bring the bombs here," Sey-Us said, in a low voice. "And be
quick about it." Thespa was quickly at his side and Sey-Us took out two of the bombs. The beast turned in their direction, saw movement, and charged.

"When I throw the bomb, stretch out, and keep your face to the ground until I tell you it's clear," Sey-Us said. Thespa gave the bombs a suspicious look.

"The gas rises," Sey-Us explained, and turned his eyes back to the beast. Its wild charge suddenly stopped and its nostrals flared as it picked up strange scents. It ambled ahead, cut lose with a bloodcurdling roar, and chanrged again. Its speed surprised Sey-Us as it closed on the No'mo sailors. Risc-Um hurried to Sey-Us as the sailors sought better cover. Thespa moved away dragging the case.

Risc-Um and Sey-Us stood facing the onrushing creature. Risc-Um raised his rifle and fired three times with no effect. Sey-Us waited for it to get close enough for the bomb to have a good chance of stopping it. He took the pin from the bomb and glanced at Risc-Um.

"When I throw this, drop and don't get up until I do," Sey-Us said, in a steady voice. Coolly, he hurled the bomb and dropped to the ground.

The bomb exploded in front of the beast as Sey-Us quickly pulled the pin and tossed the second bomb and covered his head with his arms. It exploded just behind the first and the beast's head was engulfed in dense red vapor that rose slowly into the now quiet air. Sey-Us heard short snorks as the beast began gasping, he dared a look. Risc-Um inhaled the damp odor from the soil and the dew on the plants tasted bitter as it ran over his lips. He felt the ground tremble as a loud thud came to his ears. He would have gotten to his feet but Sey-Us pressed a hand against his shoulder anticipating his action.

When Sey-Us took his hand away, Risc-Um pushed himself up. When he stood he stared at the beast lying before them. Nearly three time as long as tall, it lay stretched out twisting its head. Its mouth kept opening with labored gasps and Risc-Um saw razor teeth lining it. As

Sey-Us stood beside him, the creature began a bone snapping motion with its mouth. They could see the rise and fall of its massive lungs.

Risc-Um was disconcerted at the nearness of the beast to where Sey-Us and he had been. He looked at Sey-Us with a queezy feeling and pointed to the beast.

"That thing came a good thirty feet after the second dose of gas,"
Risc-Um said. "Don't you think that's cutting it a bit thin?" Sey-Us held a look of triumph.

"Could be. The important thing is the bombs stopped it." Sey-Us took in the scene elated.

"I told you my bombs would stop anything." Risc-Um gave him an annoyed look.

"Yeah, but you forgot to mention how long it would take. Is that thing dying?" Sey-Us shook his head.

"No, but that's easily rectified," Sey-Us replied, stooping to pick up his rifle. He walked forward, looked into the savage yellow eyes, raised the rifle and fired into the eye. The beast convulsed, roared, and began trembling in its death agony. One slight convulsion followed and it lay still beginning to stiffen. Sey-Us fired into the eye again wanting to be certain it was dead.

When he got back to Risc-Um, the sailors were emerging with doubtful expressions.

"What sort of beast is that?" Risc-Um asked.

"A morogorn. A very primitive animal thought to have gone extinct millions of years ago," Sey-Us replied, glancing at the sailors who had gathered. After a few moments staring, the sailors felt ashamed at their panic and began collecting equipment they had dropped in flight.

"A primitive animal," Risc-Um said, thoughtfully shaking his head. A sudden recollection electrified Sey-Us.

"Flaming hell! Risc-Um, do you realize Ihand-A was right?" Risc-Um turned a puzzled look to him.

"She was correct when she assumed the beast-god to be some kind of primitive animal," Sey-Us said, rapidly. "If this beast is any indication, this entire plateau must harbor such beasts. How could they have survived uncounted ages?" Sey-Us slowly rubbed his jaw, contemplating the discovery.

"That can't be true," Risc-Um protested, ignoring the grusome sight in front of him. But he knew Sey-Us was right – as always.

"The survival of these beasts was believed to have been impossible," Sey-Us said. "But we seem to have discovered that the opposite is true. That means we've made the most srupendous discovery of all time." Sey-Us' voice sounded even, but Risc-Um detected the mounting excitement.

Sey-Us carefully thought about what this would do for his prestige.
He knew Risc-Um's denial was a natural reaction. It was irrational to
disbelieve something with evidence before your eyes. Risc-Um picked up his rifle and checked to make sure the barrel hadn't been fouled then slung it on his shoulder. He motioned for the sailors to line up.

"Let's move and look for tracks," Risc-Um ordered. He turned his face to Sey-Us.

"I got a feeling we're going to meet more of your survivors, Sey-Us. Personally I don" care about any discovery. I'm here to make certain Ihand-A stays alive." Sey-Us agreed with his assessment.

"We're going to find animals definitely not to our liking," Sey-Us said, as Risc-Um moved out.

DANGEROUS TRAIL

Tracks were not difficult to follow in the daylight, and they were still heading for the mountain. They moved steadily along the stream, unaware they were moving down a slight slope. They became aware they had moved into a depression when they saw the swirling mist.

"That's an awful thick fog," Thespa said. Sey-Us noted the stream vanished into the cloud and that it did so at the deepest spot of the depression. They heard splashing as if something was wading through shallow water and then the sound faded in the gray wall before them.

"That has to be Gnok," Sey-Us said.

"We'll soon find out," Risc-Um said, and hurried on.

They were quickly slowed as the fog surrounded them. Risc-Um groped ahead until he stepped in water. He waited for the others to gather around him. The lake was a formidable barrier and Gnok'' track was at the water's edge just filling in.

"He's already across," Risc-Um said, waving his arm in a frustrated gesture.

"How are we going to get across? Swim?" a sailor asked, in a tired voice.

"Don't be stupid," Sey-Us snapped. "We've got rifles and vapor bombs to carry over there."

"I can think of only one way across," Risc-Um said.

"How?" Sey-Us asked. Risc-Um pointed alo0ng the shore at the driftwood.

"We build a raft."

"Good idea," Sey-Us said, and leaned his rifle again a stump. Risc-Um turned to the sailors.

"Let's get to work," Risc-Um said. "A raft won't build itself." He
turned and began pulling a log from the water and was joined by the sailors.

124

After an hour of lashing logs together with vine, the raft was finished. Before they embarked, Risc-Um determined to tell them what they faced. Briefly, he told them what Sey-Us believed about the jungle they were in.

"This is more than anyone bargained for," Risc-Um concluded. "If any of you want to head back to the captain now's the time." The sailors glanced at each other and looked to Thespa. He nodded and turned to Risc-Um.

"Mr. Risc-Um, none of us are going to turn tail just because we've come up against some grusome creatures no one has seen before," Thespa said, as the sailors nodded. Risc-Um felt proud.

"That makes the odds even," Risc-Um said. "These beasts haven't come across the likes of us."

"I guess that gives us an edge," Thespa said, patting the case of vapor bombs. "We've got a few surprises of our own." They seemed at ease with the situation and Risc-Um felt they had lost enough time.

"Let's get moving," Risc-Um said. They loaded the raft and lashed the equipment down. Risc-Um kept busy to keep the picture of his last look at Ihand-A from coming to mind. He suspected Sey-Us seemed to be waiting to apologize and Risc-Um couldn't take that. He knew Sey-Us never apologized, or accepted blame, for whatever fate befell anyone.

The raft was found to be too small and had to be enlarged. The lakewidening from the stream seemed to be a catchall for anything that chanced to fall into it. The lake vanished into the mist without a ripple.

"How deep do you think this lake is, Sey-Us?" Risc-Um asked.

"Ten, fifteen feet," Sey-Us replied, guessing. "The way the reeds are lined and lack of movement in the water could prove deeper on the other side. Risc-Um looked into the fog.

"We'll have to chance it and try to cross quickly," Risc-Um said.

Cautiously, the sailors stepped on the raft carrying a long pole for balance and propulsion. Yet there was barely room for the last sailor.

"Don't let the bombs get wet," Sey-Us said. "They may prove our only effective weapon."

"I'll take care of them," Thespa said, confidently. Risc-Um glanced at the crowded raft.

"Everyone ready?" Risc-Um asked.

"All set, Mr. Risc-Um," Thespa replied.

"Shove off," Risc-Um ordered. They pushed away with an awkward roll that all but tumbled the rear sailors into the water. They were saved by their shipmates grabbing hold of them. Soon they were pushing the raft in unison across the mist-veiled lake that brought on some humor. As the mist closed around them, their mood darkened as the raft proved unstable.

"Easy does it," Sey-Us said. "Hold her steady. Don't let her swing." One side suddenly became awash tipping the balance precariously, but hurried movement brought it level again.

"Keep the weight centered," Risc-Um said. "That should steady it some."

At the midpoint in the lake, the poles found no bottom to push against and no current to carry them on. They began using the poles as oars that proved virtually useless and caused the raft ro tip and spin.

"I think I see land," Risc-Um said.

"We'll find bottom soon," Sey-Us said, as motion caught his eye. "What was that?" No sooner had he spoken than the stern of the raft grated against something. They felt it was a large log as nothing could be seen.

"Flaming hell! Sey-Us exploded, as a glistening head and upper section of a large body rose above the raft. The beast was menacing as it vanished into the fog.

"Drogorn," Sey-Us shouted. "This is unbelievable." His voice broke with consternation, awe, and triumphant excitement. The dreadful specter threw the sailors into panic. Facing a large beast on land was one thing, but on water, with no bottom to push against, it was frightening. Their poles began to beat the water wildly without coordination.

The sudden shallowing gave them forward momentum and saved the raft a little longer. It tilted the raft and a sailor fell off, but caught hold of a trailing vine and slowed the raft. The huge head arced back down into the water and silently a mountain rose above the surface then vanished with only a slight ripple.

"Push! Push harder," Risc-Um implored.

"It's coming up under us," Sey-Us shouted. "We're almost to the shore."

"Psh!" Risc-Um shouted. "Or we'll be food for that thing." Their last power went into a few decisive, reckless lurches. Ten times the power they had couldn't have moved them from the great phantom that glided beneath them.

They were short of landfall when the raft shuddered from a blow and rose into the air on the back of the monster. The raft shattered sending the sailors tumbling into the water.

"The bombs!" Sey-Us yelled. "Try to save the bombs. But Thespa was barely able to save himself. Sey-Us made a desperate grab for the case, and lost his rifle. Everyone flailed furiously trying to gain the shore. As the raft was reduced to logs, one fell from the beast's back and struck one of the sailors on the head. Risc-Um saw him go under and he didn't come back up.

Looking like frantic insects, they quickly made the last few yards to shore. In the lead, Risc-Um was the first ashore and moved along helping sailors out of the water. As Thespa pulled himself onto land, he knew they had lost all of their weapons.

The drogorn teetered amid the remains of the raft. The veiling mist and shower of logs had confused its slow-witted brain. Except for that bit of luck, fewer sailors would have made it out of the water. As they got to their feet, the beast's head cleared enough for it to begin pursuit. It lumbered onto the shore as the sailors fled before it. It moved slowly until it saw one lagging sailor to whom it gave chase with portly steps. It was ungainly on land and slow, but the length of its pace made it faster than its fleeing prey.

"Move it," Risc-Um shouted, as he ran.

As they scurried away, the land rose and the mist dropped away. The heat and humidity soon added their discomfort. Risc-Um stopped on a narrow ridge that sloped down to a wide morass of soft black expanse with spots firmed under pressure of time and formed large plates. Sey-Us joined him and stared before interpreting what they saw.

"Pitch," Sey-Us said. "This was probably existing before any beast gained life. A black hole to oblivion. There are thousands of carcass entomed in it." He anticipated Risc-Um's question.

"We'll have to be extremely careful crossing it. If anyone gets stuck they will sink slowly into it." The sailors came up behind them and sank to the ground, glad to rest. Sunlight warmed the wet fur and soaked clothing as the exhausted sailors looked at the tar pit with little interest.

Behind, the ground sloped down into the motionless cloud, looking like a shroud for any that wandered into it. Materializing from it, the last sailors appeared. They dropped by the others and stretched out. Risc-Um counted the survivors and found two missing. He knew one had died in the lake but where was the other one?

"Look!" a sailor shouted, pointing. Following his arm, they saw on the far side a single figure dwarfed by distance. He raced toward a group of trees. It was the missing sailor and Risc-Um wondered how he had gotten so far away from them. From the mist behind came the beast, lumbering along but gaining on its hapless prey. All were on their feet watching the fatal play.

"Everybody remain where you are," Sey-Us ordered, as Risc-Um took a step forward. He would have gone to the sailor's aid if Sey-Us' voice hadn't expressed his authority.

"No one could reach him in time," Sey-Us said, grimly. "And if you could, what could you do? We've nothing left to fight with except our wit and knives." Sey-Us was being blunt to let them know they had to worry about themselves. They watched impotent as the horror unfolded in vexing silence.

The fleeing figure managed to get to a tree and with tenacity climbed into the lower branches. The beast paused and seemed to be smelling the tree. The tree looked like a matchstick beside the giant drogorn, its head bent down with a slow deliberate move.

"Wasn't anyone able to hold onto his refle?" Risc-Um asked, furious at his helplessness. Sey-Us gave him a grim look.

"Everything but us is at the bottom of the lake, Risc-Um. Besides, what good would a rifle be against that beast?" Sey-Us, too, felt helpless.

"If we only had a couple of those bombs, we might be able to save him," one of the sailors said.

"If I hadn't let them go, I would have drowned," Thespa said, defensively, feeling frustrated.

"There wouldn't be anything we could do if we had the bombs," Sey-Us said, sternly. "He's too far away." They didn't like what he said, but accepted it.

The drogorn's head moved until only a thread-like sliver of light separated it from the unlucky sailor. A distant scream of terror drifted across the distance as the massive head and body merged. The group drew closer together and one sailor became sick. Another sprung forward, but Risc-Um stuck out his foot and sent him sprawling on the ground. He helped him up and faced the others.

"We've got to move on," Risc-Um said. "No sense standing
around here." He knew the tar pit posed a problem and an idea came to him.

"Spread out," Risc-Um said. "Find Gnok's trail."

"We could try to find a narrower point to cross," Sey-Us said. Risc-Um shook his head.

"I want you to take the party back to the captain, Sey-Us. You can get rearmed and come after Ihand-A and me." Sey-Us regarded him with shock and knew Risc-Um had to be persuaded differently.

"I'll have more luck trailing Gnok alone. I'll leave a trail. Try to get back before I catch up with him." Sey-Us nodded.

"I can't see risking the party in our condition," Sey-Us said. "Be alert, Risc-Um. You've seen how easy this jungle catches one unaware."

FATAL ENCOUNTER

Risc-Um's main concern was to keep the rest of the party alive, but knew it couldn't be done unarmed. Reflecting about the beast-god, his mind called up a picture he had seen carved in the stage's platform. The picture was so lucid he stared across the black expanse he thought what he saw was imagination. The shouts of the sailors brought the beast into reality. The collossus they had been seeking was ambling toward them from the jungle and to the tar pit. Seeing it in daylight brought out its frightfulness. Its body was as furless as any primaloid and resembled them in everything but size.

Moving along the edge of the pit with caution made him all the more incredible. Inconceivable, too, was the care with which he carried Ihand-A. His primitive brain prized his holding for reasons it couldn't comprehend. Much as a primaloid female might have cradled her child, he carried Ihand-A's limp body in the crook of his arm. The watchers would have sworn there was design in the way his broad back was inverted between his captive and the pursuing beasts dogging him. That was until their feet was caught by the suck of the tar. These creatures were yet another species that had survived for ages on Scumm Island.

Huge, gray four-legged beasts with thick necks supporting a stubby head ending in long tapered snouts. They threw their heads back and roared as they pursued Gnok. They and Gnok were focused on each other and failed to see the observers on the crest. Gnok put Ihand-A down on one of the solid plates and turned his wrathful attention to his pursuers.

"Down," Sey-Us ordered, in a harsh whisper. All dropped behind clumps of brush and watched.

"If only I had some bombs," Sey-Us lamented. Risc-Um couldn't take his eyes from the battle that was about to unfold.

"What are those animals, Sey-Us?" Risc-Um asked.

"Unigorns. Another species that was thought to be extinct," he replied, in a classroom tone. Risc-Um had heard of such creatures before, but had believed them to be fossils and paragraphs in textbooks – until now. The party was watching a drama from the dawn of time.

"What a discovery!" Sey-Us exclaimed, drawing a sharp look from Risc-Um.

"Only if we survive to tell about it." Sey-Us glanced at Risc-Um knowing that was the truth he had to face.

Facing his antagonists, Gnok prepared for battle standing on one of the plates, luring the beasts on until one became trapped. Its weight was pulling it down as it tried vainly to extracate itself. The remaining two had followed safe paths and were closing on the waiting Gnok. He roared defiantly, ripped a large chunk of hardened tar from between his feet and flung it at the charging creatures.

"I can't believe any beast could be so strong," Risc-Um said, in awe. What surprised all of them was the force with which gnok was heaving boulder-sized chunks with such accuracy. One struck obliquely, breaking open the side of one beast's head causing it to reel,obviously hurt by the blow. Roaring in triumph, Gnok made a rapid end of the wounded beast by smashing its head in with a well-aimed chunk of tar. He then turned his full fury on the remaining unigorn, but it swung away and retreated into the jungle, and toward the hidden watchers.

Risc-Um heard a panicky murmur from the brush.

"Stay put," Risc-Um said, in a hard tone.

The beast in the tar while trying to escape only managed to sink further. Gnok ripped another huge chunk of tar loose and cast it at the struggling beast. It struck squarely on its eye sending a shower of blood over the black surface. The beast slumped to the side in fits of twitching that wracked it. Gnok roared and thumped his hands against his chest nnouncing his victory.

Sey-Us was becoming concerned for their safety.

"We've got to get away from here," Sey-Us said. "Let's start moving back to that clump of trees." The sailors quietly followed Risc-Um and Sey-Us. Risc-Um caught sight of a fallen tree that spanned a gorge and felt they might be safer on the other side. He patted Sey-Us' arm and pointed. Sey-Us nodded and they turned in that direction.

Gnok had calmed down, picked up Ihand-A and moved away from the battlefield. It seemed to Sey-Us the beast-god was moving at an angle that would take him around the far side of the gorge. By crossing the tree bridge, Risc-Um felt they could keep Gnok in sight.

It appeared to Sey-Us the third unigorn would cause them no problem as it moved almost parallel to them. It, too, had been struck by a couple of Gnok's well-aimed missiles. The party tried moving quietly, but it was impossible in the undergrowth as Sey-Us kept a wary eye on the unigorn.

"Everyone keep still," Sey-Us, whispered. They stood among the trees as the unigorn turned toward them. Without provocation, it charged and they ran.

All made it to the tree bridge except the slowest sailor. Glancing over his shoulder in terror, he ran into a low hanging branch and fell stunned and came to his senses too late. He took shelter behind a small tree, but the unigorn hit the tree snapping it and causing it to fall trapping the sailor. As the others watched, the beast eyed the tree warily, looking for its screaming victim. Seeing him, it proceeded to disembowel him. As his scream died, the unigorn pushed its head into the leaves and branches and pulled its head back with the sailor in its mouth. During this time, no one noticed Gnok transit the tree-bridge. They were fortunate in that he didn't see them. Gnok was heading for his lair with Ihand-A still unconscious in his arm.

Moving toward the tree-bridge, the weary and depressed survivors showed none of their former boldness that had been high when they dashed through the gate. They felt sorrow at the loss of shipmates and weapons, but remained Risc-Um's handpicked volunteers. Faced with an unknown peril, they had maintained fortitude that is the noble knight's salvation. This alone would have been a powerful weapon under other circumstancess. Cast away in any other jungle, they would have united their ability and skills and triumphed over jungle and beasts. But here, they knew demoralization. There seemed little use of gile and intellect against the brute force of the giant, primal beasts of this nightmare island.

Their frail knives were useless against the beasts. Their rifles and vapor bombs had sunk to the bottom of the lake along with their hope. Armed, they would have fought on, but lacking these, they were as powerless as the unigorn that had struggled in the tar. No one, even the usualy confident Thespa, felt their chances were good. Hard sullen oaths fell from their lips as they filed through the jungle. Not words of daring-do but the grudging wrathful oaths of Orangs who have been trapped through no misdeed of their own, and could see no clear way to safety. Only Risc-Um and Sey-Us avoided the pitiful abandon.

Guiding the weary party, Risc-Um wracked his mind for a strategem that would see the unarmed party back safely to the wall. Once they had rearmed, they stood a better chance of freeing Ihand-A from her grotesque master. She was his only goal and armed or unarmed, Risc-Um was going after her. Sey-Us tried to recall the path they had taken from the great wall, but during the hours of darkness there wasn't much to recall. The only logical path was to follow Gnok's path back to the stage, skirting the lake. Sey-Us felt confident he could lead them back, but must do so while they could travel in daylight. After they had reequipped, they would stand a better chance against the beasts. Sey-Us understood this as well as Risc-Um.

From behind them a crashing came from the jungle, and was getting louder.

"That thing's coming this way, Mr. Risc-Um," a sailor said, fearfully.

"Hold up a minute, Risc-Um," Sey-Us said, as Risc-Um stepped on the tree-bridge. "We've got to reach a consensus about what action to take." He quickly outlined how he could get back to the wall and his hope for the safest way. He considered it to be good if they started before darkness.

"That suits me," Risc-Um said. "All you have to do is find a way to avoid that beast behind us." Sey-Us patted Risc-Um's shoulder.

"You better get across," Sey-Us said. "There's no reason for the rest of us to cross as I think we can evade the unigorn."

As Risc-Um started across, Sey-Us glanced over the edge into a scane of unbelievable horror and looked at Risc-Um. Sey-Us knew his footing on the tree had to be certain or it would be the end of him. The floor of the gorge was covered with a slimy silt and suffocating smell of rotting flesh. There were caves and long razor faults amid which the denizens lived.

Sey-Us looked from the repulsive scene and watched Risc-Um's progress with silent concern. A feeling of relief filled him when Risc-Um stepped on the other side.

"I would have felt very bad had you fallen," Sey-Us said. "This gorge is a breeding place for the foulest things I've yet seen on this island. Take a look, Risc-Um." Sey-Us motioned for the sailors to step forward and look. As though silently summoned, a creature that resembled a brown boulder on stilt legs came creeping out of one of the caves. It seemed to be aware of the watchers because everyone thought it was staring hungrily up at them. A small creature lay warming on a sunny ledge as the stilt-legged thing moved stealthily toward it. A larger version of the thing appeared in the mouth of the cave making the stilt-legged thing think better of its action. It moved away to seek another unwary victim.

A spherical creature came along on wriggling tentacles, providing a convenient opportunity for stilt legs. It approached cautiously then pounced, evoking an unnerving sound that couldn't be described as a scream, but a screech that froze their blood. Victim and hunter quickly disappeared into a cave aith the screeching continuing for a moment before an abrupt silence filled the gorge.

"I'm not crossing that log," one of the sailors said. "Not with the like of those ugly things under me." This made Sey-Us glance toward where the unigorn was almost to the edge of the trees. It had taken time for it to career its way through the dense foliage and didn't seem to know which way to move. It stopped and sniffed for some minutes before deciding to move toward the sailors.

"Stand still, everyone," Sey-Us said, knowing the beast was nearsighted. "We may not have to cross the log if it mistakes us for rocks and trees."

The unigorn was slowly making its way through the trees, its head lifted and its yellow eyes questing for anything in its path, and it was making directly for the sailors.

"So much for trying to look like trees," Sey-Us shouted. "Let's get across the log." He began pushing reluctant sailors onto the log. Obedient to his direction, they moved carefully onto the treacherous span. They watched their footing, constantly aware of the odious things that crawled beneath them.

Moving them as fast as he safely could, Sey-Us glanced at the trees and saw the unigorn's head emerge. He grabbed a hefty rock, drew back, thought better of it and dropped the rock. Throwing at it would only antagonize the creature without causing it any harm. The sailors grouped together inching ahead toward the other side. Sey-Us had just stepped on the log when he heard Risc-Um's warning.

"Go back," Risc-Um was waving them back as he yelled. "You'll be safer on the other side. Take your chances in the jungle. Gnok's coming." He waved desperately before grabbing a vine and dropping into a slight hollow below the log.

Gnok came lumbering up, saw the sailors, and roared a challenge while thumping his chest. He placed Ihand-A in the top of a lightning shattered tree, then stormed to attack this new enemy. Still angry at the unigorns, Gnok was doubly incensed at the appearance of the sailors. The sight of the unigorn charging from the opposite side brought his anger to fury.

Sey-Us had no choice but to follow Risc-Um's example and slid down a vine into a shallow fissure. The unfortunate sailors were trapped on the log. To move toward Gnok was impossible and to retreat no less dangerous. The unigorn sensing its large enemy rushed to the edge of the gorge and bellowed a challenge acoss the span.

From their respective positions, Sey-Us and Risc-Um watched the tragedy unfold. To Gnak, anything that moved was an enemy and had to be destroyed. He rumbled his challenge and thumped his chest, seeming more interested in the unigorn than the sailors. He grabbed a moderate sized tree, snapped it in two and launched it. The deadly missile came down and tore into the unigorn's neck joined the body. The unigorn went mad with pain, bellowing in agony and thrashing wildly around. It tried to push the tree out with its forefoot. Its roars were deafening and it crushed trees and brush as blood spurted from its neck in a fatal stream. The beast fell on its side, the tree still impaled in its neck.

Gnok now turned his attention to the sailors, after announcing his victory and beating on his chest. The desperate sailors clung tanaciously to any projection on the log instead of trying to move back. Gnok had eliminated one danger but presented an even greater one. Sey-Us was astounded as he watched Gnok sink on his haunches, press his fists on the ground, and seemed to study the problem of the sailors on the log. They cried out fearfully, and two tried to move to solid ground, but fear of falling stopped them and they reinforced their grips on stubs of broken branches. They watched Gnok not knowing what to expect.

Risc-Um tried to distract Gnak by shouting. Gnok looked around, saw him, but refused to be distracted. Sey-Us tried a different tactic. He threw stones, but Gnok ignored them. Gnok stood, took hold of his foreskin, let it swell and released it. The gush of urine caused two sailors to lose their grip. One grasped madly at a nearly prone shipmate and left bloody tracks on his cheek as he fell into the decaying rot. He had no more than touched bottom when one of the tentacled horrors flashed from a cave and began to feed on the sailor.

Risc-Um watched in horror as another sailor struck, sinking to his waist and still conscious. A number of stilt legs swarmed over him tearing him to pieces. As his scream

138

died away, Gnok again lifted his penis. With a loud howl, he arced his hips forward and released the foreskin. Another sailor was knocked off and dropped into the midst of the creatures below. There ensued a battle between the stilt legs and the tentacled creatures over the fresh food.

Gnok seemed enraged that a few sailors still manged to cling to the log. It took time and careful aim for him to release his most powerful urination that sent three more sailors plunging to their doom. The bottom of the gorge was a maniacal feeding frenzy. Rising was the eerie sounds of the creatures as they fought. Any creature that became wounded quickly joined the menu.

One sailor clung desperately to the stump of a large branch. Risc-Um couldn't make out who it was because of his location. He felt furious at his helplessness, but knew there was nothing he could do to distract Gnok. Gnok lifted the log and shook it vigorously but didn't dislodge the sailor. The terrified sailor was Thespa who Gnok was now glaring at. He picked up the log, swung it, and released it. For an instant, Risc-Um saw Thespa still clutching the stump. It dropped, hit the side of a ledge and snapped in two before dropping to the gorge floor.

Gnok looked over the edge, turned, and moved away. Risc-Um was puzzled that Gnok hadn't beat his chest and roared his victory. Stepping to the edge, he found himself threatened by a stilt leg climbing the vine in front of the shallow depression. Its lidless, yellow eyes were on Risc-Um. He drew his knife and hacked at the tough vine. Before it parted, the creature had gotten close enough for Risc-Um to hear its breathing. In a last determined slash, the creature went plunging to the bottom adding to the feast there.

GNOK'S CHALLENGE

Dazed and trembling, Risc-Um determined on the rescue of Ihand-A He heard someone call his name and looked across the gorge. He hadn't ever recalled seeing Sey-Us look worse.

"I had to take cover from the unigorn," Sey-Us said, in a shaken
voice. "What do we do now?"

"You go back to the skipper, and I'll follow the beast." Sey-Us gazed at him in astonishment.

"You're going on after what you just witnessed?" Risc-Um nodded.

"There's no choice if we want to save Ihand-A. I'll be counting on you getting back with vapor bombs." Sey-Us knew it was the only help he could give Risc-Um.

"It's the only chance she has, Sey-Us. Now shove off, and try keeping yourself in one piece." Sey-Us gave a hesitant nod, turned, and hurried back along the trail. Risc-Um's attention had been on Sey-Us' departure and hadn't been aware that Gnok's hand was moving toward him. Unnoticed, the beast-god had crept back and knelt above Risc-Um. Risc-Um back into the depression and took the knife from its sheath and stabbed it into the huge palm. The beast-god jerked his hand away in surprise and rubbed the slight, but painful, wound. He glowered downward, bellowed, and rubbed his palm again. He bent down and groped into the depression quickly drawing back. He kept repeating this, not wanting to give Risc-Um a chance to inflict anymore wounds.

Becoming frustrated, he thrust his hand into the hollow and began moving it slowly against the wall. Risc-Um stabbed the hand and finger but the beast-god ignored the slight scratches. Risc-Um ducked back and fourth avoiding the hand stabbing furiously. Now he was in a corner where the hand barred him from the front of the depression. Risc-Um felt if he could cut a tendon he might have a chance to escape. He pressed against the rock, gripped the knife tightly, and readied himself for a last chance to escape from Gnok's grasp.

The prickling edge of the splintered branch brought Ihand-A slowly back to consciousness. She turned her head, saw where she was, and gazed over the jungle glade. Turning her eyes up, she saw dark green vegitation give way to the lighter sky that made the canopy a distinct horizon. Where she was and how she had come to be here, her aching body prevented her recalling. She shook with a glut of fear but her memory still failed her. She got the ache alleviated slightly by not moving.

A new giant horror filled her mind and set her to trembling. Recent events came flooding back in the clearest detail. The most clear being the glittering torches on top of the wall. She recalled her helplessness at being tied to the stage and those electric blue eyes that had examined her, the great hand that had descended followed by darkness.

She recalled short intervals of conscuousness when she was being carried through the jungle and recalled the reason for the dread she felt. Ihand-A noted she was too high to risk a jump to the ground and the height made her giddy. Looking down, she saw an odd looking serpent resting its head against the trees its eyes on her. She saw Gnok on his knees preoccupied.

Bursting out of the foliage came a grotesque double of the beast-god. It had patchy brown and yellow skin; deep set slanted brown eyes, and wiry black hair. Its body was furless and slightly larger than Gnok. Ihand-A's scream was involuntary. There wasn't room in her mind for one Gnok let alone another, and she kept screaming.

The sound of screams brought Gnok's head around and his attention away from Risc-Um. He saw his enemy, rose to his feet, and made a mad rush to defend his prize. As the serpent slithered away, Gnok gave it a kick to hurry it on its way. His rage became focused; he beat a quick tattoo on his chest, and moved to the attack.

As Gnok closed with his enemy, the dark beast clenched massive fists and his eyes never left his adversary. His lips rose in an animal snarl revealing yellow stained teeth. The huge beasts stumbled backward as their bodies impacted, taking them off balance. Gnok was the quicker and it seemed his new enemy would go the way of the unigorns. It would be a battle to the death, as were all battles on Scumm Island. This one would would be more savage for they were of the same breed and brutality would rule.

Gnok roared as he quickly hit his opponent on the side of the head, stunning him but failing to drop him. His opponent roared defiantly and moved on Gnok, whose hands flashed up to grip his throat. Not even this larger adversary could hold out long against such a determined grip. The battle was not only ferocious but extremely savage. The dark one fello on his back bringing his feet up hard into Gnok's groin and pushed. This brought Gnok off the ground and he crashed over the head of his opponent and rolled close to the edge of the gorge.

The dark one dove for Gnok but misjudged and found himself rolling to where his head and shoulder jutted over the edge. Gnok shook his head, groggy from the impact.

"Get up," Ihand-A yelled, in support of Gnok. She felt she wouldn't survive long in the dark one's captivity, and preferred Gnok's more gentle captivity. Him falling prey to any of the awful beasts inhabiting this island would mean her death, something she didn't care to think about.

Both had regained their feet and roared challenges at each other. The beast-god flung himself past flashing fists, receiving heavy but ineffective blows. The dark one lunged against Gnok and they slammed against the tree in which Ihand-A lay. It snapped under the impact and crashed into the undergrowth. This cushioned her impact but she lay stunned under a large branch.

Gnok and his opponent were grappling for an opening when the dark one fell over a log and Gnok was quick to take advantage. He took no time to roar as it had failed to intimidate his enemy but moved with deliberation. He had checked his rage as the dark one regained his feet. Their eyes locked on each other, they circled, wary, as they closed. His arm flashed out and gripped his foe's throat, twisted it, squeezing fiercely. Gnok relased his grip and leaped aside to avoid the vicious kick at his genitals.

Gnok quickly landed a number of blows against his enemy's head and he seemed to sag from the pounding and was dazed at the force of the attack. Gnok closed in, diving impetuously into his foe his hands again locking on his throat. They fell in a tangled struggling heap. The dark one got a leg against Gnok's chest and thrust, but his coordination was off. Gnok was pushed back but was able to grab the leg that pushed him giving him the advantage he had been waiting for.

The extended leg was quickly twisted flipping his adversary onto his stomach. Gnok leaped astride his back pinning his shoulders to the ground. He grabbed his ears and started slamming his face into the rocky ground. Ihand-A could see the dark one had lost. Nothing could have withstood such unvented fury for more than a few minutes. The dark one's face was becoming a pulpy, bloody mess. Pieces of flesh clung to the rock as blood spattered over the undergrowth.

Gnok stood over the inert form, put his foot on the victim's head and gave a vicious push. He ponded his chest exultantly and roared as his defeated foe quivered in weak spasms. The dark one convulsed and began stiffening. Gnok bent down with rumblings of pleasure, took hold of the hair, lifted the face and turned it to Ihand-A shaking it. She hadn't seen the conclusion of the battle. Flagged emotions, combined with pain and sickness from what she had witnessed had plunged her back to unconsciousness. Pinned beneath the branch, she lay as still as the dark one.

She had kept his attention from Risc-Um, who had been a spectator to the combat He realized Gnok had bettled his own kind before. It seemed to Risc-Um that gnok had worked out a proficiency in combat that appeared to work better when he wasn't trying intimidation. He had pulled himself over the edge in time to become fascinated by what was happening. He took cover in the undergrowth and watched the contest. When he saw the tree fall, he felt that might be a chance to get Ihand-A. He hadn't gotten close to her when the battle ended. He looked on as Gnok lifted the branch from her and lifted her to his arm.

Risc-Um began planning a course of action, noting that Ihand-A hadn't seemed to be hurt. Her only chance of rescue now relied on his skill to keep up without provoking Gnok's unpredictable nature. Risc-Um knew there would be no help until Sey-Us returned, but felt grateful that gnok had forgotten about him. Gnok's interest centered on Ihand-A. He lifted the branch from her, tossed it aside, and looked at his hard fought for prize. As he lifted her in his hand, he made encouraging sounds as he gently placed her in the crook of his arm. He turned from the field where he had fought for her.

Risc-Um, concealed in the undergrowth, noted a clear resolve in Gnok's withdrawl. Feeling safe, Risc-Um felt he would make straight for his lair. No longer worried by the small things that had chased him past the tar pits the unigorns had forced him into. Having won another battle, he was taking his blonde prize home.

"Risc-Um." He returned to the edge of the gorge and saw Sey-Us.

"I thought you had gone."

"I couldn't miss such a battle. I had been hoping that if Gnok had been beaten you could have gotten Ihand-A." Sey-Us lifted a coil of vine.

"I would have used this… for something," Sey-Us said, shrugging. He had no idea what they could have done being separated by the gorge. For the first time, Risc-Um felt a bond of friendship for Sey-Us, provided he could get past his insufferable, egotistical attitude. True he had a habit of getting his people into trouble, but he never gave up on getting them out of it. Risc-Um poined to the vine.

"That might prove useful. Leave it. Now get back to the skipper. You know I'm going to need help." Sey-Us hesitated with a sad look.

"I feel bad about leaving you to go after that beast alone and unarmed."

"There's nothing else to do, Sey-Us. We already agreed to do it
this way. I'm the only one in position to trail Gnok."

"But –"

"But nothing. If I get a chance to get her away from him I'll take it. but I'm counting on you to return with help. I'll leave a trail on this side. And do me a favor."

"What, Risc-Um?"

"Don't get chewed up." Sey-Us regarded him wondering if it might be the last time he would see Risc-Um.

"Good luck, Risc-Um." Sey-Us turned and set off jogging through the steamy jungle. When he saw the mist shrouded lake, he abruptly realized that less than two hours ago that was where Ihand-A's rescue had became a disaster. He moved to the left following the stream and avoiding the fog where death waited for the unwary.

Risc-Um set about his grim task. He scrambled among the trees moving cautiously, making certain of Gnok's line of travel, then set a pace he felt satisfied with. He kept glancing over his shoulder knowing it was dangerous not to watch your back. He came to the edge of the battlefield and looked over the tree and took a long long look at the body of the dark one. Carrion birds sat on the head plucking at a bulging eye as more flocked for the feast.

Turning, Risc-Um saw a stilt leg appear over the edge of the gorge. The odor of blood from the unigorn and the dark one would draw the things from the slime pit and quickly moved off. Sey-Us had gotten away just in time, he thought. Risc-Um shuddered at the sounds of the savage fighting over the carcasses as more of the vile creatures made their way out of the gorge.

He shook off his revulsion and set off on the trail of his large quarry. Gnok seemed incredibly clean compared to the foul things in the gorge. As it stood, Risc-Um could count on himself alone to rescue Ihand-A. That gave him a feeling of hopelessness. It took his strong will to oversome that and concentrate on what had to be done. He followed Gnok, ready to take advantage of any chance that presented itself. Risc-Um knew he was trusting to luck.

SAFE RETURN

The jungle was ancient and smelled dank, making Sey-Us wonder how many times it had died and regrown. He wished he had time for study. Although botonay wasn't his expertise, it would be interesting to find out how old it was. After what seemed endless hours following the stream, Sey-Us noticed the undergrowth was giving way to the tall grass where the stage stood,but he couldn't see it yet. The grass was waist high away from the cleared circle around the stage and Sey-Us' overtaxed feet slowed him as he neared the wall. He had to stop for a brief rest. The grass screened him along with the shadows on approaching night.

He felt extraordinary lucky to have evaded the denizens of the jungle, but fatigue was an enemy he couldn't overcome. It was growing dark when he saw the stage and wall ahead of him. The shadows made his slow approach hard to distinguish even from the top of the wall. Many eyes were scouring the jungle looking for the rescue party. At the gate, sailors stood ready to push it shut if need be. Other torches moved among the huts looking for any sign of trouble from the natives.

A sailor on the wall spotted the lone figure coming out of the grass and before he had gotten to the stage.

"It's Dr. Sey-Us," a sailor shouted, pointing. "Sey-Us is back." There was a rush to the gate. Mai-Us stepped through and waited. Torches trailed to the left and right of the gate then clustered around Sey-Us. A few sailors looked expectantly into the jungle for the rest of the party. From Sey-Us' point of view, the torches from the wall seemed to be streaming out the gate. Sey-Us waited until the curious questions faded to silence. The skipper and Pablae stepped before him.

The silence became an answer as no one followed him from the jungle. Bewildered expressions were turned to

Sey-Us as Mai-Us stepped beside him and slipped an arm around Sey-Us' sagging shoulders.

"Lean on me," Mai-Us said, and helped him through the gate and sat him down on a wooden bench. Pablae stood with a worried look.

"Where are the others?" a sailor asked. Mai-Us glanced at the sailor.

"That will have to wait," Mai-Us said. "He's exhausted. Get him some food and drink."

"That sounds good," Sey-Us said, wearily. "Keep an eye out for Risc-Um. If he's lucky he'll be coming in a hurry."

"Where's Ihand-A?" Pablae asked, a cold feeling growing in him. Mai-Us turned an annoyed look to him.

"I said wait," Mai-Us said, sharply. "He needs to refresh himself."

While the orange juice flask emptied against Sey-Us' lips, the skipper and sailors regarded his torn clothing, matted fur, and cuts with grim expressions. They waited to hear what had happened to their shipmates. Mai-Us retrieved the flask after measuring its contents with a generous eye. With the last swallow, Sey-Us shivered and wiped his mouth with the back of his hand, which was something Sey-Us didn't usually do.

"I sure can use the food, Mai-Us. I don't think I've ever been so hungry." Mai-Us sent a sailor to get food. The sailor backtracked not wanting to miss anything Sey-Us said, but Mai-Us saw him.

"Move it." Mai-Us roared, at the errant sailor, who quickly set off.

Sey-Us sighed and stretched out on the bench his spirit reviving. He glanced around and saw the anticipation on the sailors' faces.

"There's no easy way to tell of the disaster that befell the party,"Sey-Us began. He felt sorrow at the loss of the
148

sailors and unknown fate of Risc-Um. This was a new experience for him. He had had people in danger before but had extracated them with minimal loss. What had occurred this time was unprecedented. He told it simply.

"Everyone but Risc-Um and I was killed. We know Ihand-A is alive. Maybe I should say was, since I don't know what's happened since Risc-Um set off to try and rescue her. They could both be dead in that nightmare jungle." He paused and looked around.

"I need volunteers to go back out there with me and find them, if they're alive. Who will come with me?" The torchlight reflected in their brown eyes as they turned to the ground. They didn't quite understand what Sey-Us had told them.

"They won't be coming back?" a sailor asked. Sey-Us sat up and looked at them.

"I don't know," Sey-Us replied. "That Risc-Um and I survived was accidental. That white furless beast some of you glimpsed carrying Ihand-A off is only one of what lives in that primal jungle. We weren't expecting to run into anything like them." The sailor brought him food as Sey-Us struggled to compose himself.

After eating, Sey-Us retold the tale sparing none of the gory details and culminating in the final encounter on the log. He wanted them to get mad, but they were shocked into silence. Sey-Us waited a few minutes, allowing them time to think.

"I want you to know what you'll face when we go after Ihand-A and Risc-Um. I've held nothing back. The decision rests with you."

"Only you and Mr. Risc-Um…" The sailor let his voice trail off, embarrassed by the implication. Sey-Us and faced him.

"How was it possible that Risc-Um and I survived when your shipmates died? Is that what you want clarified?" A lot of the sailors' expressions answered his question in silence. Sey-Us nodded and proceeded to explain how Risc-Um and he had been trapped and sought refuge while the sailors had refused to move off the log. He told them of Risc-Um's narrow escape from Gnok's grip. They listened and remained silent after he finished.

"Neither Risc-Um nor I expect sympathy. We done what we had to and that was to keep trying to save Ihand-A> Risc-Um used only a knife to stand against Gnok. He was brave as your shipmates were." He paused and let them condier his words knowing they must understand what they would face in the jungle.

"If I had kept a closer watch on the vapor bombs we might have all been safe, including Ihand-A. Now Risc-Um is tracking Gnok alone, and I came back for help. Risc-Um put himself in danger standing in the open and warning the others to go back as Gnok came toward the log. On the side I was on, the other beast was approaching. If they had gone forward, came back, or stayed where they were, there was no way to save them."

"I know you and Risc-Um done all you could," Mai-Us said, sighing at the loss. "You couldn't have done anymore." Sey-Us looked to Mai-Us and spread his hands.

"But I brought us to this island. I led the volunteers into the jungle without considering what we might encounter. If I hadn't made it back, and something happens to Risc-Um, you would never have known what happened." Mai-Us nodded.

"We would have given you up for lost," Mai-Us agreed. "After sending out a search party – that may not have returned either."

"Risc-Um and Ihand-A have a good chance if we go to help them," Sey-Us said, emphasizing his words. Pablae turned a sad look to him.

"We'll probably never see sither of them again," Pablae said, sadly.

"Flaming hell! You know Risc-Um's no quitter, and neither am I. Are any of you just going to give up onRisc-Um?" He clasped Pablae's shoulder.

"You can bet we'll see them again," Sey-Us said, and turned his face to Mai-Us. "I want a case of vapor bombs brought here, Skipper. I'm going out at first light. Now who's going with me?"

"I'll go," Pablae said. Sey-Us glanced at Mai-Us.

"If I can't get younger, stouter, volunteers, you and I will be the
only ones going," Sey-Us said, challenging the sailors as he watched them. "Is anyone else going with Pablae and me?" Every sailor stepped forward. Some chose casually, others recklessly, according to how each reacted to their hesitancy.

"I'll go."

"Count me in."

"No fun sitting here guarding those dumb natives."

"I owe Mr. Risc-Um."

"Ihand-A done some sewing for me once."} Having made up their minds, they took on sober expressions having no illusions about what they would face once through the gate. Sey-Us was a reminder of what had happened to their shipmates and effectively quelled their swagger.

Mai-Us and Pablae was waved back by Sey-Us.

"I've got enough volunteers, Skippers. You and Pablae pull the same duty. Stay here and make certain that gate is open when we return."

"I'm not wore out like you, Sey-Us," Mai-Us said.

"That's true. But I know the way through the jungle." Sey-Us shook his head.

"The mountain's the only landmark. I'm not about to stay and let others go blundering out there like I did. It's no easy path through the jungle, Mai-Us, and I have the experience." Mai-Us looked annoyed.

"I see you're not going to change your mind," Mai-Us said. "The lead is yours." Sey-Us ignored Mai-Us' irritated tone and turned his attention back to eating as he gave orders.

"I want everybody to have plenty of ammunition. There are ten bombs to a case. I'll carry two and divide the rest between the others. I found a ford south of the lake so we can avoid that path."

"Will these bombs knock out those monsters?" a sailor asked. Sey-Us nodded.

"One slows them down, two puts them out. Even Gnok can be stopped by a couple of them."

"You need to get some rest, Sey-Us," Mai-Us said. Sey-Us looked at him with a grimexpression.

"I doubt Risc-Um is getting any rest, Skipper." Mai-Us nodded and slipped a slice of fruit into his mouth.

"How are you going to get around that gorgr, Sey-Us?" That made him consider a seemingly impossible problem.

"I believe the stream might solve that problem, Skipper." Sey-Us
didn't care to push his luck, but there was no choice.

"You need to rest before starting out," Mai-Us said.

"I couldn't sleep."

"I didn't say sleep, I said rest. Loose some of that tension you've built up." Pablae overheard the captain and Sey-Us and got an idea. He stepped to them and they turned their eyes to him.

"Captain, why not bring the witch doctor up here and ask a few questions?" Pablae suggested. "He might be able to tell us something about those beasts. If he refuses, I know a friendly way to persude him to talk." It was then Sey-Us noted the absence of the natives.

"Where are they?" Sey-Us asked, curious. Mai-Us hadn't seen the witch doctor or chief for sometime, and no native had presented themselves since they heard gunfire.

"I knocked the chief out," Pablae said, with satisfaction. "He just kept jabbering and I figured he was up to no good. It looked like he was about to stop you and Mr. Risc-Um from going through the gate. When the witch doctor saw what I done he didn't say a thing. I had them put in a hut under guard." Mai-Us and Sey-Us couldn't help grinning.

"After that, the rest got quiet," Pablae added. It was like they expected trouble and wanted to make themselves invisible."

"I wonder where they went?" Sey-Us asked, uneasy.

"The females and little ones are in the huts," Pablae replied. "We hear sounds now and again from them. As for the warriors, there aren't many hiding places this side of the wall." Mai-Us had a confident look.

"Without the chief and witchdoctor, they won't cause any trouble," Mai-Us said, in a matter of fact tone.

"You believe the possibility of Gnok returning will keep them docile?" Sey-Us asked. Mai-Us nodded.

"They feel they don't have to attack us," Mai-Us replied. "They believe Gnok will take care of us. After all, we were cocky refusing a sacrifice to Gnok, and then hounding through the jungle." Sey-Us thought about the beast-god.

"I think you're right, Skipper. Gnok's unpredictability could draw him back for retribution." Mai-Us had experience dealing with island natives. Each tribe had a rudimentary intelligence he slowly learned to understand.

"One thing, Sey-Us," Mai-Us said. "Should Gnok return, the

natives will want to see him exacting his revenge, but they won't get

in his way." Sey-Us looked grave.

"He has no reason to return," Sey-Us said.

"He would if Risc-Um manages to get Ihand-A away from him," Mai-Us' words stopped the sailors in whatever they were doing. Mai-Us popped a slice of fruit into his mouth.

"Seems to me he has to hunt for food," Sey-Us said, recalled his theory and decided to confide it to Mai-Us. "You should have seen him fight, Skipper. Gnok's more than a dumb animal. Granted he's one of nature's leftovers, but in that huge brain is a spark of intelligence. Ihand-A is special to him because she's different. He took care of her, saved her life." Mai-Us emitted a skeptical snort.

"She is special to him, Skipper," Sey-Us emphasized. "You can't believe any of the female natives would have been treated the same." The more he said, the more sound his theory became in his mind.

Mai-Us silently conceded that the local females had been treated less gentle from what he had heard from the natives. They had been amazed when Gnok had carried Ihand-A off. Mai-Us felt he hadn't done with other females.

"He saw the difference," Sey-Us continued. "He probably hasn't the dimmest conception of what the difference is, and has no idea what to do with her. But the fact remains that he's protecting her." Pablae and the sailors regarded Sey-Us with amused looks as they went about their preparations. Sey-Us saw their looks and motioned for Mai-Us to came closer.

"We've got to get Ihand-A away from him," Sey-Us said, in a low voice. "Once that happens, I don't think Gnok will be the same. He'll yield to his desire to get her back."

"Sounds convincing," Mai-Us said, unconvinced, but willing to give Sey-Us the benefit of the doubt. "In my opinion, the idea that beast is intelligent isn't worth the rust on the No'mo's rudder. I think you're conceding too much to him. He's attracted to Ihand-A because of her fur. All he's seen has been natives."

"You're right, Skipper. She is something different and he'll eventually tire of her. When he goes for food, Risc-Um will be nearby and get her." Mai-Us shook his head.

"You're too imaginative, Sey-Us."

"We'll see, Skipper." But he wasn't confident that Risc-Um might get Ihand-A. He would have to overcome Gnok's strength and cunning.

"I wish I was doing more for Risc-Um. Instead, I'm sitting here
wasting time while he's out there alone."

GNOK'S LAIR

Gnok followed no particular trail but left his presence clearly impressed on abused bushes, snapped trees, and depressions in the soil. Risc-Um had less difficulty following him than he had anticipated. Even without the obvious marks, he would scarcely have been mystified at the direction of travel. Gnok made a lot of noise in his ponderous stride that became the leading indicator that Risc-Um used to follow through the dense jungle. It was such an immense help that Risc-Um's pace became liesurely.

Gnok seemed in no hurry and that led Risc-Um to believe there were no other beasts nearby. A moment of thought about the beast-god's pace meant the area was devoid of menace. There were trails that intersected, but Gnok moved ponderously on.

Risc-Um's tracking became so smooth that he miscalculated and came dangerously close to Gnok. The sight had him dive for cover when Gnok abruptly stopped and looked behind. After a moment, he resumed his pace. Risc-Um knew his only chance of rescuing Ihand-A, alone or with help, relied on his common sense and good fortune. If Gnok suspected he was being trailed, it was impossible for Risc-Um to guess how he might react, although he had examples to go by. So he maintained a safe distance after his close encounter.

Following was easy enough without taking any chancves. In spite of his caution, Risc-Um exited one side of a clearing as Gnok passed out the other side. He hadn't had a glimpse of Ihand-A in quite awhil and he chanced a quick look from the cover of a tree. He saw her lying limply in the crook of Gnok's arm. He felt she was all right but was only guesing. In any event, she made no move while he could see her. She might have been in a sling as the great arm compensated with every step and shunt of his body. Her fur was matted and the jumpsuit had torn loose exposing her shoulder.

Passing the far side of the clearing, Risc-Um found the vegitation less dense, the ground sloped downward and now slanted up through a tangle of vines. Trees stood alone and taller with undergrowth cluttering around their trunks.

By late afternoon, Risc-Um was within sight of the purplish-black rock of the mountain and it was clear Gnok was heading for his lair that would probably be in the most inaccessable part of the peak. The path leading up seemed passable to only the large climber and nothing that would attract other animals.

The afternoon gave way to early evening as the odd pursuit continued. Risc-Um clung doggedly to Gnok's track until the trail turned steeper and led through a field of gray boulders. His body ached from falls, stinging slaps from branches, and hunger. The worst was that his feet and legs felt numb from walking, but he continued along after Gnok.

After a detour, Risc-Um came across a large outpouring of water from the mountain. An opalescent spout had cut a gutter with its discharge into a wider chute that that led to the jungle below. At first, it made no impression on Risc-Um, but an idea was quickly born. It brought renewed energy to his weary body as he realized he was looking at the mouth of the stream that ran into the lake and flowed over the plain to the outside of the wall. He was considering this as an avenue of escape as he rounded a large boulder and found himself close to Gnok. His haste for cover brought tortured protests from his spent, aching muscles. He got behind a spur of rock as Gnok looked over his shoulder.

Peering out, Risc-Um noted Gnok had halted on a great flat rock encompassed by a vertical curving ridge. A sapphire pool lay ahead of the beast-god and that was where his attention was focused. Risc-Um noted the suspicion expressed by Gnok as he watched the dead calm water that at one point came within a few feet of the serrated cliff. This puzzled Risc-Um because there was no origin for the pool, no feeder ran into it, but a slight eddying motion meant a natural drain, an ample outlet. Just why Gnok was focused on the pool, Risc-Um could only guess.

Higher up, a jagged façade surrounded the front of a gaping cave that was a dead end. There would be no other way out after passing the pool. What was he so suspicious of in a backyard pool? A slowly moving shadow in the water caught Risc-Um's eye. Whatever was rising from the depths held Gnok's attention.

A wide, yellow-green head, capped on either side with light gray eyes, slowly rose from the water and confronted Gnok. Its thick, snake-like length vanished into the pool. Gnok quickly put Ihand-A on a ledge out of reach of the coiling horror as it twisted higher causing Gnok to retreat.

He was able to dodge the first vicious strike, leaped forward, and roared into the thing's face. Risc-Um had never thought to hear a roar with a distinct trace of fear in it. As it echoed from the cliff, he beat his chest and moved to battle. Risc-um never thought he could see Gnok with anything but revulsion, was only a breath away from a supporting yell. He knew what Ihand-A's fate would be if Gnok lost this battle.

Ihand-A's shoulder appeared bright against the dark rock as she lay oblivious to what was happening. The excitement Risc-Um felt made him feel like cheering, but his common sense held sway. Growling fiercely, Gnok stormed to the assault. Some place beneath the surface, the water beast had firmly anchored itself giving it greater force to absorb Gnok's charge.

Gnok fought with hands and yellowed teeth and his feet they proved a defense unequaled. They gripped the erose surface and continually withstood the tremendous pull of the powerful coils as the slithering serpent wrapped the column-like legs. It was trying to pull Gnok into the pool where all the advantage would belong to it. Gnok roared and smacked at the weaving head.

Unlike Gnok's earlier adversaries, the water monster had only a slight his that was intimidating and a warning of danger. Gnok fought with baited breath and an occasional grunt. His teeth snapped visiously at the coiled body he held in one hand while keeping the slashing head from striking him.

Risc-Um could see neither beast gaining an advantage over the other. For long minutes, the coils appeared to tighten their hold in an increasing grip of death. Gnok's teeth tore great chunks from the writhing body while he desperately kept his grip on the serpent's head while making attempts to get hold of its lower jaw.

Risc-Um realized this wasn't going to be a short contest, he decided to try to get to Ihand-A. Before he made a move, the end came abruptly and almost silently. So quiet was it that Risc-Um had no warning it was over. Gnok stooped slightly toward the serpent's head, spread his legs as far as the confines of the coils allowed, and grabbed the head with both hands. He pushed the head back while pulling the body toward him. The loud cracking of bone was what Risc-Um heard.

With a series of moves, Gnok won another triumph in his domination of the lost world of Scumm Island. The water became alive as the serpent's body writhed and lashed in its death agony. The coils dropped from Gnok's legs and formed a twisting mound around the lifeless head Gnok now stomped on. Gnok growled lightly and almost fell over. He propped himself by placing a hand against the cliff. He was so weakened of breath and strength that he couldn't step away from the serpent. Gnok trembled in his abhorrence for the creature he had just slain. When Risc-Um saw Gnok was too taxed to move, he realized the beast-god had limitations.

When he revived, Gnok picked up Ihand-A and placed her in the crook of his arm and moved laborously into the cave. Risc-Um was quick to follow. For the first time since the chase began Risc-Um felt no fear of being seen. He knew Gnok was exhausted and boldly moved quietly from rock to rock. He put his hand on his knife and considered an assault on Gnok, but discarded the idea as suicidal. Those great hands might have spent their strength on the serpent but theyt were still powerful enough to snap him in to. Demurely, he fell back to hiding and again and bracing for what he believed would be hours of waiting. In spite of fatigue, Risc-Um had to remain alert for the moment luck might provide a chance to get to Ihand-A.

He remained in shadow and watched Gnok's final ascent to an open ledge. He put one foot slowly in front of the other as he plodded up the steep slope. Risc-Um had no difficulty distinguishing the boulders in the twilight of the cave. He marked out a trail to follow believing he could move up the slope without much trouble.

Standing on the wide shelf, Gnok put Ihand-A down between his feet and drew a deep labored breath. His strength seemed to return with every filling of his lungs. His eyes got some of their glitter back and his arms began to swing until they raised to pound on his chest. A roar of triumph rose from deep within him.

Looking at the open ledge, Risc-Um noticed an abrupt change in Gnok as he had turned his eyes skyward. He caught sight of what Gnok was watching. A large winged creature soared through the sky. Gnok bellowed loudly and Risc-Um saw Ihand-A move and sit up. Hesitantly she looked up at the sound above her and screamed. Gnok stilled his voice and looked down at her.

In the glow of the sunset, Ihand-A appeared as a light shadow against the rock. Gnok stuck out a finger and touched the fur of her bare shoulder, rubbed it, and seemed fascinated by her. Ihand-A tried moving away with a chocked sob but her clothing caught on a spur of dirty fingernail and the jumpsuit tore open revealing more blonde fur. Gnok touched her again, caressing her, then tugged on her clothing. He pealed a part away, rubbed it, and sniffed it. Ihand-A sobbed again.

Risc-Um was moved to action from his hiding place and began

moving up the slope. He could no longer wait for Sey-Us to return and knew he had only himself and luck to count on. His muscles were strained far beyond normal service and he fell more than once as he moved toward the ledge. Once he fell back to almost where he had started, being stopped when he impacted a rock that knocked the breath from him. He clung to it for a time then started for the top again.

He wondered why Gnok hadn't reacted to the noise he had made in his falls but didn't have long to ponder the question. Looking up from behind a boulder that hid him, he saw Gnok peering down in puzzlement. He pressed himself against the boulder expecting Gnok to come and take a look. Gnok moved back to the ledge.

Risc-Um strained to make it up the incline feeling the need for caution had passed. He tried to think of a way to distract Gnok so he could get to Ihand-A and escape before the beast-god could be roused.

Gnok was looking into the cave when he heard Ihand-A scream. He spun to see the winged beast lifting her in its talons. Risc-Um saw his chance and summoned his last reserves of energy. He pulled himself to the top in time to see Gnok grab the huge wings and begin his destruction of the creature. It was too one-sided to even be considered a fight, although the beast drew blood from Gnok by using its sharp beak. Gnok began tearing the fragile body into bloody pieces, diverting his attention from Ihand-A.

Using the distraction, Ihand-A got to her feet stumbled and fell. She rolled to the lip of the ledge and Risc-Um took what he coinsidered might prove his only chance. He sprang to his feet, sprinted to a corner rock, and softly called her name while keeping a wary eye on Gnok.

"Ihand-A." She looked quickly around, unable to see him in the shadow. He moved into the open and she crept over to him.

"Risc-Um? Is it really you?" Behind Gnok's back, he pulled her to him and she embraced him. They whispered like children in an ogre's house.

"I kept hoping you would come."

"I'm here now." She turned her eyes up to him.

"

Don't let him touch me again." He put his hand on the hilt of the knife telling himself he would keep her from that ordeal as he looked for a way out. Glancing over the edge, he saw the pool below and knew that could be their escape.

"Ihand-A, we're going to –" Risc-Um glanced up as Gnok finished his task of destruction and flung the bloody remains to the rocks below. He caught sight of them standing together and roared. Risc-Um moved Ihand-A close to the edge.

"We've got to jump," Risc-Um shouted. Gripping her hand tightly, they leaped from the ledge into the dark infinity below. The placid water rose to meet them looking like a solid surface until they plunged in feet first.

RESCUE

The stun of hitting the water was sudden, dropping them through the semi-darkness that made it impossible to judge the height of the water over their heads. It exploded in foam and poured over Ihand-A caressing her in a warm serene woumb. She had prepared for a shocking chill but the water amazingly was warm. It assauged her bruised and battered body, revived her, pulled exhaution from her and made her feel clean again. Her slim figure showed as a flickering pearl in the green calm.

She had sucked in a deep breath before impact and held it. They hadn't went very deep when she saw Risc-Um swerve obliquely to bring their dive to a stop, caught her arm, and they floated up. She bobbed beside him filling her lungs until she was breathing normally.

"Are you all right?" Risc-Um asked. He floated beside her blinking his eyes to free them of water that clung to his eyelids.

"I feel fine now that I'm away from him."

"Can you swim?"

"Of course, Risc-Um."

"We've got to get moving or he'll have us both real soon." Risc-Um's tone was steady but she couldn't see his expression of dread as he looked up at the ledge.

Gnok, because of his species age-old fear of water, had to take the long way down and was almost down the slope by the time they hit the water. Using his hands and feet, he was descending at a velocity that would have landed any four-legged creature fatally onto the jagged rocks.

Risc-Um guided them to where the water eddied into the submarine gutter and told her what they had to do. It made her uneasy but the thought of Gnok coming made her fearful.

"I'm ready. Just stay close, Risc-Um." He gave her hand a squeeze.

"I'll be with you all the way back to the wall."

Gnok made a wild leap and came down hard, his blue eyes ablaze with rage as he raced to the lip of the pool. Risc-Um became aware of just how close he was and urgently hastened Ihand-A along. When Gnok roared, Ihand-A emitted a desperate cry of fear almost becoming mad at the prospect of becoming his captive again with freedom so close at hand.

"Dive," Risc-Um shouted. Ihand-A pulled herself under with Risc-Um desperately following. Ihand-A had to surface just short of the gutter's mouth, Risc-Um behind her and alert. Gnok had either figured out their destination or his eyes were sharp enough to distinguish their shapes under water. With a loud vehement roar, he limbered for the mouth of the gutter. He was almost close enough to thrust his hand down and cut off their escape.

"Dive," Risc-Um yelled, alarmed.

Ihand-A plunged into the warm depths and the mouth was within reach. In the clear water, she aimed for the mouth as her tattered clothing fluttered as she gought with her arms and legs to escape. She glanced up and became terror stricken when she saw the great hand reaching for her. At that instant, Risc-Um grasped her hand letting her know he was with her. The current took hold with an irresistable force and carried them rapidly forward. Ihand-A didn't try to resist the current and let herself go limp and took the bumps as it carried her along. She stretched her arms over her head and moved along like a piece of driftwood.

There were no sharp obstructions in the chute, but before they emerged, she was twisted and her knee slammed painfully against the side. Darkness engulfed them as they

164

dropped from the chute into darker waters. Ihand-A's lungs had hardly began to object against the stale air when her head emerged in a froth and she found herself in soft phosphorescent water between sheer rock walls whose tops vanished toward the stars. She bobbed on the surface taking deep breaths and looking for Risc-Um.

"Risc-Um, where are you?" A sickly feeling overcame her as fear of being alone in the jungle seemed to be true. She twisted, straining her eyes, trying to locate him. Then he bobbed to the surface and sucked in air. He swam over to her and put a hand on her arm. She closed her eyes as a flood of relief swept over her.

"Take it easy," he said, confidently. "This stream will take us most
of the way back." She let the water wash over her as they floated
along, the current keeping them moving at a steady rate.

"Gnok will have to follow jungle trails and that means we'll win this race, Ihand-A" She gave him a dubious look that he missed in the dark.

"What if we don't beat him?" she asked, apprehensive. She had been through an ordeal she had no propensity to repeat.

"He don't like water," Risc-Um replied. "And I can't say I blame him after what I saw in that pool." She relaxed at his assurance and drifted along with her head resting on Risc-Um's arm. She took hold of his hand as a question occurred to her.

"What are you doing out here alone and unarmed? And why did you take such a risk to save me?" He related what had befallen the party and she was horrified at the loss of the sailors because of her.

"I hope Sey-Us made it back. All these beasts, why he could have…" He let his voice trail off not liking the possibility. She reached out and touched his cheek causing him to wince sharly.

"You're hurt." He glanced at her in the slight glow.

"Gnok made a grab for me as I washed down the chute." He changed the subject by downplaying his role. There had been no way to minimize the risk he took to save her. She tenderly touched the scar again sending a surge of pain throu his face.

"Brave Risc-Um. And I haven't got enough rags left on my body to cover a grape let alone give you a bandage. I owe you that, at least. If we can slip ashore, maybe I can find a leaf to cover your wound. My modesty can't count for much now." She tried keeping her voice evern, feeling she was about to cry, but giggled. That was the curative dose both needed and Risc-Um grinned. Both were physically and mentally exhausted. Risc-Um had regained a little strength from the water and relief from tension. He turned his face and kissed her, until they sank. Ihand-A broke the surface spluttering and laughing as Risc-Um popped up beside her.

"I couldn't think of any other way to celebrate your escape," he said. "More importantly, I want you to know how I feel about you." Her smile faded as she thought of her terrifying time with Gnok, and knew he was following. She was so tired she would have sunk like a rock had Risc-Um not been with her. She was only now beginning to comprehend how famished she was. She knew danger lay in wait along their escape route. But she was elated to be free when only hours before she had considered herself dead.

She leaned to him and returned the kiss.

"I couldn't help that," she said, softly. His hand was on her cheek, and in the slight glow from the water, as they drifted.

166

"Do you realize neither of us is using common sense?" he asked, not feeling impelled to move faster.

"You have to admit, Risc-Um, feeling contentment is more agreeable than being rational." She turned her eyes to the stars.

"Don't ever say that in front of Sey-Us." They laughed and continued the relaxation neithewr had known since the natives had taken her.

"Have you any idea of our position, Ihand-A?" She caressed his unwounded cheek.

"My position is with you. You know where we're going so I trust your navigation."

"Your confidence is humbly appreciated. You might think differently after I tell you what sort of beasts we may run into." He told her what Sey-Us now believed about the island. As he talked, the cliffs gave way to jungle, and the current's flow seemed at abate slightly.

"Do you feel strong enough to swim?" Risc-Um asked. "Don't strain, just move with the current."

"Sure. Why?" Risc-Um's sense of danger was growing.

"We're not far from that lake, and we can't afford to waste anymore time." The inactivity was also urging him to action. He was certain Gnok was wasting no time following them.

"I can swim for awhile," she said, rolling on her stomach and taking slow strokes.

"That's good, Ihand-A."

"I'm letting the current do the work, Risc-Um." In the obscure jungle darkness, her arms and legs functioned in gentle motion and she felt it was pleasant.

"Let me know when you're tired," Risc-Um said. "We've got to be more alert." He was becoming concerned as they neared the lake. Away from the mountain, surrounded by jungle, he became more alert.

"I want to get us out of this jungle as soon as possible. We'll go on land before we get to the lake. I don't want another encounter with that beast." He shuddered as he recalled the pursuit of the beast.

The thought of walking made Ihand-A realize how weak she was and knew she had to tell Risc-Um.

"I don't know how long I'll be able to walk. I'm not very strong
from not having anything to eat in over a day."

"I can carry you if I have to." She turned a stern look to him.

"You're in no condition to carry me. You haven't eaten or rested in almost two days." Risc-Um remained silent, but determined to succeed.

"I can carry you for five miles, but the distance around the lake is less than a mile."

"Or until you fall on your face," she mumbled.

Risc-Um wanted to get them to the gate knowing they wouldn't stand much chance evading Gnok in the jungle. He knew he didn't have the stamina to move quickly bearing both their weights, yet he knew he would tap into a reservoir of strength when needed. The unwavering confidence she had in him helped depress the fear of recapture, and that was to be avoided by all means.

"I wonder if he's following?" Ihand-A asked.

"I've been wondering the same thing," Risc-Um replied, aware he hadn't heard any sound of a large beast in the jungle.

"He has to eat. We must have gotten far enough away to be safe."

"He makes his own trail through the jungle, Ihand-A, and is probably heading for the gate."

"I can't believe he would all that way just for me. That's not basic instinct for an animal." She wasn't certain if she was trying to convince Risc-Um or herself.

"Gnok isn't just an animal, Ihand-A." Her mind rejected his conclusion because she couldn't accept that such a creature had intelligence.

"He has to be hungry. Hunger is the most basic instinct." Risc-Um nodded.

"You have to stop thinking of him as a dumb beast, Ihand-A." His tone expressed apprehension that filled her with dread. It was probably a theory Sey-Us had dreamed up, she thought. But why was she surprised? Risc-Um had been on other expeditions with Sey-Us.

"That's a big assumption, Risc-Um. Is it your idea or one Sey-Us came up with?" He remained quiet for a moment giving her time to think. She had to purge her bitter feeling and determined to keep her demanor.

"It was awful being his captive. You can't know about those huge hands unless they've touched you. He poked me as though he were trying to understand. And the way he looked at me!" She couldn't go on putting her fear into words. What Risc-Um had said haunted her.
He knew he had to break her fixation before it ran too long.

"Let's concentrate on what we're doing. If we weren't so tired, we wouldn't be talking this way." Risc-Um had to get her mind on what had to be done to ensure their safety. She pulled close to him as they again floated along.

Moving through the opalescent water, the dark jungle slipped past and faded in the distance. The current was beginning to slow, making their headway tiring. Risc-Um, in spite of her protest, made Ihand-A get out of the water and rest. Once she complied, he became sharply alert. He was aware the jungle seemed quiet, but it was a place where the unwary could meet a sudden, violent end.

Back in the water, Risc-Um felt safer.

"See how the stream is widening?" he asked, after a few moments swimming. A distant crash brought dread welling up in them.

"Are we close to the lake?" Ihand-A asked, and shuddered. It was clear what was ahead of them as they could see the gray-white wall of mist that stood out clearly in the darkness. Risc-Um caught a vine, slipped an arm around Ihand-A, and pulled them up on the bank. They rested briefly before starting to walk, skirting the mist.

"I have to rest," she said. Risc-Um picked her up and she acknowledged her exhaustion be leaning slackly against him and drifted into a light sleep. He moved away from the lake into the crowd of trees and undergrowth. His head occasionally brushed against her face as he ducked under low hanging branches.

She awoke when he stopped and put her down against a tree.

"I need a short rest," he explained. They were surrounded by jungle that Risc-Um knew hid the giant beasts. After a few minutes, he stood erect and picked her up.

"We'll keep on until I have to rest again." That he did twice and Ihand-A couldn't sleep. At their third stop, Ihand-A noticed they had returned to the stream.

Back in the water, they found ample current and left the mist covered lake behind.

"What's that noise, Risc-Um?" He stiffened as far in the jungle they heard an enormous crashing and growls. He glanced at her and didn't want to alarm her.

"Maybe a beast hunting," he replied, feeling it was Gnok. "I don't want to face one of them on such unequal terms. Let's get moving." Ihand-A felt he presumed it to be a particular beast and that filled her with fear. She began swimming almost frantically, finding the threat renewed her strength. The rest she had gotten while Risc-Um had carried her had refreshed her. When Ihand-A slowed, Risc-Um had her take hold of his belt and towed her. From ahead, he heard a sound that made him jubilant. It was the last of their water trail.

"We're almost there, Ihand-A. Remember I told you the stream divided into two chutes?"

"Yes."

"That noise is water rushing through those chutes." The sound grew as they drifted closer.

"This is going to be more difficult than the first chute," Risc-Um said. "But we don't dare delay getting to the trail and walking would take too much time. Are you ready?" He knew she had been prepared as he had spoken.

"Yes," she replied, mustering her confidence. "I'm not woorled – very much. Just stay close to me." He gave her shoulder a gentle squeeze.

"I'll be right behind you."

They saw the phosphorescent spume glowing and enlarging ahead of them.

"Relax and let the current do the work," He said, confidently. From far behind, they heard another loud crashing, but it seemed farther than the previous one. But the sound of the water made Risc-Um uncertain of that, knowing the jungle muffled sound and could deceive one about distance.

The roiling phosphorescence eddied about them and spurted them down the chute. It seemed to be over almost before it began. In their brief descent, bioth were battered. Pulling themselves onto the bank, Ihand-A saw Risc-Um's left arm hung limp and bleeding while her thigh was streaked with blood from knee to hip. They lay gasping for air.

"Is your arm broken?" she asked, too fatigued to feel her own pain.

"No, just numb from being beaten against the chute. But you're sure hurt." He could see the dark blood staining her fur.

"And poor me doesn't have a bandage." She glanced at her practically nonexistent clothing then to Risc-Um, who couldn't see her face. She looked into the jungle and her hope surged. In the distance, she saw the glow of torches from the top of the wall.

"That's what matters, Risc-Um," she said, raising her arm, her voice filled with elation. Barely visible, he saw the dark bulk of the stage and the shimmering yellow glow of welcome puncturing the
jungle darkness.

GNOK'S RAGE

It seemed so incredible that Risc-Um took a double take to make certain what he was seeing was real.

"They're waiting for us, Riscv-Um. We're safe." As she flung her arms around him, he knew better than to believe they were safe. That would only come when they were back on the No'mo. He put his good arm around her and shared in the relief that they had made it back. Getting to their feet, they hung onto each other as they made their way toward the gate. He held his arm under her shoulders to keep her weight off her cut leg and they hobbled on.

As they moved, Ihand-A clearly heard a faint crashing in the direction of the mountain, but it was subdued. She put it out of her mind. Being hurt and exhausted, she tried helping herself to make it easier on Risc-Um in the final stretch to the gate. Seeing the gate open, Ihand-A felt she could now put the nightmare of the past days behind her. Once past the gate, she believed Sey-Us wouldn't let anything happen to her. She was confident in the ability of her boss and benefactor. It didn't cross her mind that Sey-Us had been the one who had gotten her into this situation.

Risc-Um felt a little relieved being close to the gate, but his instinct told him Gnok wasn't far behind and coming on steadily. He wanted to be on the other side of the gate and see it closed and secured against Gnok. They were safe from the emerald hell they had traversed. As they approached the glow of the torches, one though filled Risc-Um's mind. They were alive. They had lived through a bizarre adventure neither had dreamed possible. Now that it was almost over, it was difficult to believe it ever happened. But Risc-Um had some insight into Gnok and, unfortuneately, his boss. He knew the clash between Gnok and Sey-Us was far from over.

There had been so much talk about the white, furless beast that Pablae felt a little edgy. It was just so much hot air, as far as he was concerned. A bunch of sailors flapping their gums about something they hadn't seen. But Pablae had to admit that something had taken Ihand-A and killed his shipmates. Something that had Risc-Um in the jungle chasing after it. The idea of a knowedgable person like Sey-Us talking about such an animal being intelligent was bilge wash.

Just the same, he felt it wise to keep an alert watch as he ambled through the torchlight. Pablae stopped beside the gong and gazed into the dark clearing below. To the right of the stage, his sharp eye caught a slight movement. As his vision focused, an electric excitement flowed through him. Unsure until they came within the glow of torches, he turned quickly and looked down.

"Captain. Dr. Sey-Us. Mr. Risc-Um and Ihand-A are coming out of the jungle," he shouted. "They're back! They made it." His shouting brought everyone to their feet and racing for the gate. Pablae was down off the wall and out the gate as the others crowded around the gate. Sey-Us and Mai-Us quickly followed Pablae, Mai-Us chewing on a piece of fruit. A plethora of sound erupted from the sailors.

Coming past the stage, Sey_Us saw a tired, staggering Risc-Um with Ihand-A leaning against him. Her almost total lack of attire popped Sey-Us and Mai-Us' eyes open and they drew their dignity quickly to the surface. Pablae was first to reach them and help Ihand-A, relieving Risc-Um of the burden.

"Bring blankets," Mai-Us ordered. Two sailors rushed out the gate carrying blankets. Sey-Us quickly wrapped Ihand-A but Risc-Um refused a blanket.

"Give Mr. Risc-Um a hand," Mai-Us told the sailors, and they helped him along after Sey-Us and Ihand-A passed through the gate.

Sey-Us now supported Ihand-A as the sailors faced them.

"Didn't I tell you Risc-Um would bring her back?" Sey-Us asked. "He's a shipmate you can be proud of." He spoke with admiration and none would dispute his praise. Risc-Um had certainly earned their respect. Sey-Us turned his attention to getting Ihand-A down on one the native mats. Glancing at Risc-Um, Sey-Us shoulders squared straighter than ever. Mai-Us was giving orders for food and drink be brought. Risc-Um noted that no one had thought to close the gate and no one was guarding it. The vision of Gnok rushing through unhindered alarmed him, but his first concern was Ihand-A.

"Give her medical aid, Sey-Us," Risc-Um said. "And get some hands to close the gate. Gnok's following us and can't have been far behind."

Mai-Us came over with a flask of orange huice and handed it to Ihand-A She felt she had never tasted anything so delicious, took several gulps, and handed it to Risc-Um. She gave an apprehensive look at the open gate and trembled. After Risc-Um finished drinking, he turned his eyes to Mai-Us.

"I brought her back, Skipper." Mai-Us clasped Risc-Um's
shoulder.

"I never doubted you wouldn't," Mai-Us said, pleased.

"Mr. Risc-Um done good," Pablae said. "He's a real hero." Sey-Us nodded as the sailors gathered around Risc-Um and patted his shoulders. But Risc-Um was keeping a wary eye on the gate.

"Sey-Us, get the gate closed," Risc-Um demanded. "Unless you want that beast coming through it, bar it." Mai-Us glanced at the gate and immediately understood Risc-Um's concern. He gather some sailors and went to the gate.

Ihand-A stretched out on the mat covering herself with the blanket. Relaxing made her aware of the worsening pain in her leg.

"Can you look at this cut on my leg, Doctor. It really hurts." She winced as a sharp pain shot through her leg.

"And check Risc-Um's arm and the cut on his cheek. Sey-Us looked to Risc-Um who nodded at Ihand-A.

"Take care of her," Risc-Um said. "I can wait. He stood to emphasize his condition. Sey-Us moved the blanket from her leg and moved a finger along the cut in a gingerly manner.

"Bring a flashlight, Pablae," Sey-Us said.

With the flashlight on the wound, Sey-Us examined it.

"It's an ugly gash, Ihand-A. You're going to need stitches. We've got to get you to the ship." He turned his attention to Risc-Um and began examining his arm and cut.

"A going away present from Gnok. I told you I'm fine." He tried jerking away but his expression of pain said otherwise. Sey-Us gave him a satisfied look.

"You're going to need stitches, too," Sey-Us said, ignoring Risc-Um's behavior. "And a sling for that arm." He handed each two capsules from a bottle he took from the medical chest.

"These will help alleviate the pain," Sey-Us said. They washed them down with drinks from the flask. Ihand-I painfully stood and limped over to Risc-Um, leaned her head againg his shoulder, and broke down releasing her pent up fear.

"Are we really here, Risc-Um? Or is this some horrible dream?" Sey-Us gently put an arm around her shoulders.

"You're among friends, my dear. You'll soon be safe on the ship," Sey-Us said. Risc-Um pressed her against him.

"Get it all out, Ihand-A," Risc-Um said, softly. "It will make you feel better." But she was asleep against him. Pablae and Sey-Us put her back on the mat and covered her. Risc-Um saw Sey-Us looking
from him to Ihand-A like a proud father.

"That's the only time she's given in to her emotions," Risc-Um said.

They had become so distracted at the return of Ihand-A and Risc-Um, the sailors hadn't noticed the returning natives. The whole tribe cautiously moved out from their hiding places and the females peered from the huts at the reunion by the gate. One female appeared and others began coming from their huts. What they were witnessing was unbelievable to them. Gnok's sacrifice had been returned. A few warriors found the chief and witch doctor ungarded and told them what had happened.

The chief and witch doctor soon stood on the ceremonial stage with a few warriors as others dared take torches and climb the wall. Mai-Us saw this and knew he had to stay on top of the situation and ordered them to stop. The sailors noting this, moved quickly to act as a protective cordon around Ihand-A, who was sleeping. It was obvious the natives meant to cause no trouble, they were simply bewildered. They began a low, monotone chant quite unlike their earlier savage intoning.

"Gnok. Gnok. Gnok." It went on slowly and continuously.

"Where is Gnok?" Sey-Us asked, dourly. "Ane what's he up to?"

"Who cares?" Risc-Um countered. Sey-Us understood Risc-Um's attitude, but it was clear he didn't understand that Sey-Us' plan might come to fruition. Sey-Us now believed the golden opportunity he had been secretly hoping for might occur.

"Now that Ihand-A and you are safe, I propose to capture Gnok alive," Sey-Us said, without fanfair. Those sailors' mouths that didn't fall open simply scratched their heads. They couldn't believe Sey-Us meant what he said.

"You can't be serious," Mai-Us said, with an incredulous expression. "You must be crazy, Sey-Us. Haven't you had enough trouble from that beast?" Standing beside Mai-Us, Risc-Um gave Sey-Us a defiant look.

"I'm not crazy," Sey-Us said. "I mean to take him alive. But dead and stuffed if necessary. In any case, I'm taking him back." Mai-Us shook his head sadly knowing Sey-Us couldn't be disuadedd.

"How do you plan to accomplish this feat?" Mai-Us asked. Sey-Us had planned for this all along and felt he had an infallable plan.

"Vapor bombs," Sey-Us replied, confidently. "If he comes, as I'm certain he will, we'll drop them from the top of the wall. Once he's out, we'll chain him and take him to the No'mo." Risc-Um snorted loudly.

'I don't think there's much chance of that," Risc-Um said, skeptically. But his voice didn't betray the foreboding he felt about those sounds they had heard in their flight. It might be the only way to talk Sey-Us out of his madness. Risc-Um had no doubt Sey-Us meant to try and pull off his scheme.

"Not much chance of getting at him on that mountain," Risc-Um continued. "His lair's on the highest peak. Nobody could get at him without committing suicide." Sey-Us got a presumtuous look.

"You did, Risc-Um," Sey-Us said. "And you got Ihand-A away from him. Earlier you felt certain he was following you back here, now you say he's where no one can get him. If he comes, I'll take him alive."

"What reason would ha have to come here?" Risc-Um asked, dreading Sey-Us' answer.

"It seems clear to me," Sey-Us said, glancing at ihand-A. "You took something from him, and he'll be wanting it back."

"He's never going to lay his foul hands on her again," Risc-Um said, angrily. "I'll not let you use her as –"

"Bait, Risc-Um?" Sey-Us asked. "I don't have to use her in that manner. You should know by now that I will do nothing to jeopardize Ihand-A. But we've started something I'm going to finish." Risc-Um and Mai-Us exchanged helpless looks.

Sey-Us had picked up the gut instinct from the way Risc-Um had reacted to the open gate and his statement that Gnok was only a few miles behind them. Sey-Us was determined to have his way. He was the expedition director after all.

"I don't want to hear more objections," Sey-Us said, in an authoritative tone. The sailors glanced at each other with apprehension. Sey-Us knew them to be brave and loyal, but this was an unusual siruation.

"I have my hand closing on Gnok. We don't need any bait! The instinct of the beast should compel him to remain safely on his mountain top," Sey-Us said, trying to explain his newly developed psychology of Gnok. "But anger at the loss of his prize are far stronger than his inherent instinct. He's the god of these natives, king of this island. We came here and interfered in his, until now, uncallenged domain. So he'll be coming. For revenge if nothing else. And we'll be waiting for him. I want you Risc-Um, to have some sailors help you get Ihand-A to the boats and return her to the ship."

CAPTURE

Risc-Um watched two sailors lift the mat with Ihand-A on it and start for the beach. Risc-Um turned to Sey-Us.

"We'll see you back on the ship, Sey-Us, I hope." Risc-Um followed the sailors.

On the wall, the natives' slow rhythm suddenly erupted into a loud, horrified wail and their torches began arcing through the air.

"Gnok! Gnok!" they shouted, pointing beyond the wall. A loud thumping, followed by an angry roar, announced Gnok's arrival. Risc-Um glanced over his shoulder then urged the sailors to move faster.

"He followed her!" Sey-Us exclaimed. Although he had expected it, it still surprised him.

Looking at the gate, Risc-Um realized Gnok had put Sey-Us' plan onto the trash heap by showing up before he was ready for him and leaving no time for preparation. But Sey-Us was determined to play the game the way circumstances dictated and wouls watch for any advantage.

"Get some men on the wall," Sey-Us shouted. Mai-Us, Pablae, and several sailors formed a rearguard to protect the sailors taking Ihand-A to a boat. They and Risc-Um were hurrying along as the others moved back toward the gate.

Peering through the narrow slits in the gate, the torchlight gave a dim surrealistic picture of Gnok pressing against the gate. His deep roar pulled a communal groan of terror from the netives. The lip between the gate doors enlarged when Gnok slammed against it, pushing back the sailors and natives pressing against it. The log holding the gate closed began to bend making a loud snapping sound as the tremendous weight of the beast concentrated against it. The space bewteen left and right was steadily widening. With an enormous rending of the bottom of the gate, Gnok got his foot between them. His hand came through above his foot and moved to the log that was splintering. A prodigeous thrust of his mighty shoulder and the gate burst open.

Sailors and natives fled in panic as fear of Gnok swept their ranks. The sailors and captain screened Risc-Um and Ihand-A as they stopped at a boat. Risc-Um was worried they might not make it to deep water soon enough.

Sey-US grabbed two bombs from the open case and headed for Gnok, only to be caught up in the fleeing mob and carried along a short distance. Gnok stood in the gate roaring triumphantly as he ripped the left door from its hinges lifted it over his head and threw it. It crashed down on four natives crushing them. The other side he smashed to splinters until it fell. Gnok turned his icy glare on the scurrying creatures below. Natives flad toward the imagined safety of their huts, the sailors toward the beach. The beast-god was looking for one particular person, and he didn't see her. He sniffed the air and headed for the beach.

"I've got bombs!" Sey-Us shouted, helpless with rage. He tried desperately to disengage himself from the surging mass. His first close look at Gnok stunned him. The size of the beast was unbelievable. When he had seen Gnok at the log he hadn't looked quite so large, but he had been on the far side of the gorge.

"Don't run! I've got bombs." His voice was lost in the din of panic and Gnok trendled past the gate and began destroying the village.

Over the huts the early light of dawn made itself more visible as shouts and sounds of running foretold a day of tragedy. Torches were dropped beside dying fies scattered around the cantral plaza. Some warriors flung away their torches and fled into huts while others took to the undergrowth. Gnok ripped off roof after roof, bent down and peered inside, and became more enraged with each failure.

Sey-Us managed to escape the mob and moved widely behind huts flanking Gnok until he stood directly in the beast-gos's path. Holding a bomb in each hand, he remained concealed, but as he began to move, several sailors joined him carrying more bombs.

"He hasn't seen us," Sey-Us whispered. Gnok stepped to the next hut and ripped the roof off.

"Let's move toward the beach," Sey-Us said. "See if we can lure him from here. When he comes after us, I'll toss a bomb, then each of you use one as needed." Sey-Us was devising a plan as events flowed.

"The huts are close enough to deflect the vapor cloud and we need clean shots if they're to be effective." The sailors moved back with no sign of their former panic. As Sey-Us moved, he kept a wary eye on Gnok. He shredded the roof of another hut and discovered natives cowering inside. One by one, he picked them up, squeezed the life from them, and flung them violently against the wall. Sey-Us shuddered as the terrified screams reached his ears.

Sey-Us deliberately stepped into the open and began walking
toward the beach. Gnok paid him no attention, continuing his methodical, deadly search. When Sey-Us topped the slight rise, he saw Risc-Um and an awake Ihand-A in a boat moving toward the No'mo. The growing light showed the sailors and Sey-Us standing alone.

"Come and see if you can get us," Sey-Us yelled. "Let's decide who the boss is here." Gnok's eyes turned to Sey-Us and he saw the boat. Thumping his chest, Gnok headed for the beach and directly at Sey-Us and the sailors.

It seemed to Sey-Us that Gnok had seen Ihand-A in the boat and wasn't going to let anything keep him from his prize. Sey-Us motioned for the sailors to form a line behind him as he stepped forward and Pablae was suddenly beside him clutching two bombs. As Gnok closed on Sey-Us, the first bomb struck directly in front of him. As the casing shattered, the red vapor enveloped the beast gods upper torso. Sey-Us moved forward, threw another bomb, and stepped back. Gnok came through the second cloud and the third exploded in his path less than fifty yards from Sey-Us.

Everyone in the boat, except Ihand-A, was watching Sey-Us close on Gnok. Gnok was losing to the gas. A deep recriminating roar, that altered into a fit of coughing, escaped him as his head swung from side to side. He clutched at his throat as his forward motion was now a drunken stagger. The gas wasn't acting as quickly on Gnok as it had the more brutish animal. Sey-Us was certain he was fighting the effects of the gas.

"Look at him!" Sey-Us shouted, in triumph. "I told you the bombs would stop him." Sey-Us was in a fever of excitement as he took the last bomb from Pablae and stepped heedlessly forward. This one broke against the beast-god's chest. In the morning light the vaporizing liquid glistened as it spilled down his chest. Gnok struggled blindly on and swung his arm that came close to striking Sey-Us, who quickly moved out of the way. As he did so, he stumbled and fell back on the sand.

Gnok stretched a hand toward a frozen Ihand-A, a plea for help. Unable to lift his feet, he fell forward and struggled to breathe as he crashed face down on the beach. His incredible bulk lay immobile. Mai-Us made a dash to where Sey-Us had fallen.

"Are you all right?" Mai-Us asked, seeing the triumphant look in Sey-Us's expression.

"I'm fine," he said, getting to his feet and looking at his captive.

"Now we have him, Mai-Us." Sey-Us rubbed an elbow that had hit a rock when he fell, but he was so elated he didn't feel the pain.

"We better get back to the ship before he comes around," Mai-Us said, fully expecting Sey-Us to agree. Sey-Us shook his head.

"Send some of the crew to the ship, Skipper. Tell them to bring chains and tools to make our guest secure." Sey-Us eyeing his trophy as Mai-Us gave him an incredulous look.

"You intend taking this monster back to civilization>"

"Flaming hell, Mai-Us! Why shouldn't I? He'll be out for days from the dose of gas he inhaled. But get to it. Every minute counts," Sey-Us said, giving an order.

"Sey-Us, you don't know –"

"But I do," Sey-Us snapped, and immediately regretted his tone. "Listen, Skipper, I know what I'm doing. The crew will have to build a raft to float him to the No'mo where he'll be confined in the forward hold in chains." Mai-Us was quick to note Sey-Us seemed unable to keep his fascinated gaze from Gnok. Sey-Us was figuring what size chains was going to be needed. Mai-Us looked at Gnok and shook his head.

"No chains will constrain that beast for long, Sey-Us," Mai-Us said, in a grim tone.

"He was responsible for the death of ten of the crew," Sey-Us said, pointing to Gnok. "Do you want him to get away with that?" Mai-Us felt it prudent not to reply, feeling it wouldn't be good for anyone to have a falling out with Sey-Us.Sey-Us squared his shoulders looking satisfied. He now had things his way and that meant no compromise. As master he played the part well.

"We'll put more than physical chains on him," Sey-Us said, confidently. "He's now a fallen god who will learn humility to the civilization that's beaten him. Animals can be taught to fear their masters. That will cower him so much our chains will have no trouble holding him." Impetuous with high spirits, he rested a hand on Mai-Us' shoulder.

"Listen, my friend, you don't comprehend what a capture like this will mean. We've taken a living beast – a legend of the Forgotten Zone – and from it we'll be wealthy." He was trying hard to pull Mai-Us out of his somber mood. He raised his hand and arced it in front of them.

"In a few weeks our story will spread around the world. Once it becomes known, our names will be instantly recognizable."

"I understand what you're hoping for all of us, Sey-Us. I just feel you"e taking only sorrow and death back.""He turned a stern look to Sey-Us.

"Mark my words, Sey-Us, the responsibility will be yours alone." Mai-Us walked off down the beach and reluctantly gave the order Sey-Us had issued. The crew brought the chains and began assembling the raft.

CIVILIZATION

The following afternoon, Gnok remained unconscious and confined in the forward hold. As the No'mo lifted anchor, the remaining natives gathered on the beach to watch their only purpose in life sail away across an unknown sea. What would become of them? There seemed nothing left for them. All they had was their lives that seemed useless without their god.

Sey-Us and Mai-Us were on the bridge plotting the shortest course back to Isense. Risc-Um was doing what had to be done to secure the ship for the voyage while Ihand-A was laid up in her cabin. The No'mo's engines were thumping furiously with an urgency to get home. It vanished into the fog bank and the island vanished. A few hours later, it moved under a clear sky and through a calm sea. Mai-Us brought her up to twenty-two knots and the fog was soon out of sight. The weather remained hot and humid enough to discomfort the crew once more.

A few days later, Sey-Us was considering the report he would radio to Cari-Us and scanned it to make certain he put in only enough detail to stir the scientific community's curiosity. It was standard Sey-Us ploy, used successfully on his previous expeditions. He had always had a flair for the dramatic that brought him animosity from his fellow scientists. That made no difference to Sey-us and he remained as rascally a person as he always had.

On the bridge, Risc-Um stood gazing over the ocean, a bandage covered his cheek and his arm remained in a sling. Mai-Us was plotting on the chart and seemed concentrated on it.

"I'm glad we're away from that island," Risc-Um said, breaking the silence. "I was beginning to think I would never get the stink of that jungle off me." He was feeling better now that Ihand-A was safe in her cabin. Mai-Us looked up from the chart.

"What do you think of our cargo?" Mai-Us asked, interested in Risc-Um's opinion. It had been him and not Sey-Us who had beaten the beast-god. Risc-Um turned to Mai-Us and shrugged.

"I think Mai-Us will try to teach him a few tricks then sell him to a circus or zoo for an unbelievable sum. As for Gnok, he's going to have to learn to behave himself." Mai-Us shook his head with a doubtful look.

"Do you really believe that beast is going to remain docile?" Mai-Us asked. "If you do, you have more faith in Sey-Us than I can muster."

"I don't think it will ever be tamed. Not even Sey-Us can do that. But as long as he's restrained, I don't think he presents much of a threat." Neither had seen Sey-Us come on the bridge.

"Would you have us dump our fortune over the side, Skipper?" Sey-Us asked, causing them to turn to him.

"I can't help how I feel, Sey-Us," Mai-Us replied. "That beast is a vicious killer and having it onboard makes me nervous, and that's understating it."

"What can he possibly do, Skipper?" Risc-Um asked. "He's chained in the hold." He quickly wished he had kept his mouth shut.

"I'm not talking about now, Risc-Um. Here he is harmless. But how is he going to react once his feet are back on solid ground?" Mai-Us said, stubbornly.

"Don't worry, Skipper. By the time we get to Isense, he'll know I'm the master," Sey-Us said, confidently. "I'll be able to control him." Risc-Um wanted away from this conversation.

"I'm going to talk to Ihand-A," he said, and left the bridge.

The smell of the sea on the light breeze was placid as Risc-Um and Ihand-A walked by the forward hold watching the sunset. Standing by the rail, Ihand-A felt the need to get something said that had been bothering her.

"In a strange way I feel sorry for that beast," she said. Risc-Um turned a surprised look to her.

"After what he put you through?" She glanced at him and nodded.

"I guess you would feel some sympathy," Risc-Um said. "He saved your life and for that I'm grateful." Risc-Um felt the depth of that emotion as deeply as Ihand-A.

"I wish Dr. Sey-Us had left him on the island," she said. "It somehow just doesn't seem right taking him like this." Risc-Um snorted impatiently.

"Convincing Sey-Us to leave Gnok on the island could only have been accomplished if he were unconscious," Risc-Um said, sourly. "He wouldn't have listened to reason from anyone. You should know by now how stubborn he can be." Just as Ihand-A was about to reply, Sey-Us came over to them, stopped, and looked into the hold.

"How is our guest behaving?" Sey-Us asked, turning to Risc-Um.

"Just the same, Sey-Us. He just sits there and stares at the sky. He's been inactive since that gas wore off." Sey-Us nodded with a pleased look.

"Seems he learned who the boss is.

"I wouldn't be so sure about that," Risc-Um said, feeling Sey-Us was becoming overconfident. Ihand-A folded her arms and faced Sey-Us.

"Why didn't you leave him on the island?" she asked. "It would have been better for all concerned." Sey-Us feigned a shocked look. He had been expecting this from her before now.

"I would have thought that you, of all, would understand the significance of such a capture," Sey-Us said. "That beast's worth a lot to science."

"Please, Dr. Sey-Us! Don't try fooling me with the value to science," Ihand-A said, sharply. "Gnok's more valuanle to you than science." She turned abruptly and started for the bridge. Walking past the hold, her foot caught in a coil of rope. She fell, rolled to the hold and fell through.

Ihand-A screamed as she fell, attracting Gnok's attention. He recognized her and opened his hand and caught her. He regarded her for a moment' growled softly, which made her cringe against his finger. Her fear of him wasn't as great as it had been and it surprised her. He lifted her up to where Risc-Um and Sey-Us stood looking down in horror. He lifted Ihand-A high enough for them to get hold of her arms and lift her back to the deck.

"do you realize what he just done?" Ihand-A asked, looking at Sey-Us with disbelief at her unexpected release. Sey-Us was just as stunned as she was.

"I saw it, but I can't believe it," Risc-Um said, slipping an arm around her waist.

"It's as if he comprehends his situation," Sey-Us said, awed. This was something beyond anything he had ever come across.

The crowd was pouring into the University Arena to see what the secretive Dr. Sey-Us had brought back this time. The learned professors, such as Cari-Us, had been skeptical but remained mum on Gnok until they could study him thoroughly. They had been embarrassed before by Sey-Us when he had brought back what they had considered impossible.

Behind the newly erected stage, a deputy made way for Ihand-A following her with an admiring look he reserved only for the best looking females. Returned to civilization, Ihand-A felt very different than when she was Gnok's captive on that far off island. She wore a long blue gown that covered her feet but left her shoulders bare. She stood quiet waiting for what she knew was to come and dreaded it.

Risc-Um stepped beside her and it felt as if he had always been there. She put her hand on his arm and gave him an anxious look.

"I don't want to get too close to him, Risc-Um," she said. "I feel sorry for him the way Dr. Sey-Us has him trussed in chains and caged."

"You shouldn't even be here," he said, knowing he was right. Yet he, too, had given into Sey-Us' insistence.

"He said he needed us to tell our story of what happened," Ijand-A said, wishing she could forget the experience. Risc-Um was disappointed with her. After her annoyed outburst on the No'mo, he felt she had won her independence. But it had been the only time she had expressed disapproval at Sey-Us. None of them had mentioned the incident again.

Risc-Um felt uncomfortable in the white dinner jacket that acented his slender body. But that special air that was Risc-Um came through.

"I don't mind being here as long as it helps. Right?" she asked, lamely. "Besides, I can't forget what Dr. Sey-Us did for me. And we have to think of the families of those sailors who died." He didn't care for her first statement but agreed with the motive of the latter.

"I guess so," he replied. "I can't bring myself to believe everything's going to go as smoothly as Sey-Us thinks. I've got my trouble at hand feeling."

"What sort of feeling?" Sey-Us asked, stepping from behind the curtain where he had been making a last expression of the captive's chains.

Sey-Us looked almost laughable, Risc-Um thought, all decked out in a black jacket with a pink flower stuck in the lapel. This was the eager, mindful Sey-Us intent on enhancing his reputation and turning a profit at the same time. He felt both of equal importance.

"You two don't look like the Ihand-A and Risc-Um we took off Scumm Island," Sey-Us said. "Ihand-A, you look splendid in that gown. Do you like it?" She rubbed her hands on the fabric.

"I love it. But it was awfully expensive," she replied, with modesty. But her eyes sparkled as she recalled just how wickedly expensive it was. Sey-Us patted her arm.

"After what you went through, you deserve it," Sey-Us said. "All of us, and I include the crew of the No'mo and their families, are embarrassingly rich, and this is just the beginning, my dear."

"Well I'm not going to like being rich if I have to wear clothes like this," Risc-Um complained, pulling at the collar with a stiff finger. "It's the sort of clothes my father wanted to see me in."

The deputy was holding reporters and photographers at the back door, and they kept trying to slip past him.

"Yes, yes, I know all of you," the deputy said. "But I've been given no authority to allow you in yet." They called to Sey-Us until he finally went to greet them. He stopped and raised his hands for silence.

"You can let them in, Clitho," Sey-Us said. The deputy was glad to let him handle the noisy, pesty press. They followed Sey-Us back to Risc-Um and Ihand-A.

"The agents of the press are here to talk with you both," Sey-Us said, proudly. Risc-Um turned an annoyed look to Ihand-A.

"Did you know about this, Ihand-A?" Risc-Um asked, angered at being cornered by Sey-Us' convenient memory lapse.

"Not until now," she replied, softly. "It must be necessary if Dr. Sey-Us arranged it." Risc-Um shot a killing glare at Sey-Us who ignored it and proceeded.

"The press is waiting to hear your stories," Sey-Us said, looking like a proud father.

"You're the first mate of the No'mo?" one of the reporters asked. The question was especially irksome to Risc-Um as they knew very well he was.

"That's right," he replied, in his gruffest voice.

"You were lucky he was able to rescue you," another cut in quickly. "How did he do it?"

"We heard you had more trouble than one person could be expected to handle, Risc-Um," another interhected, before Ihand-A could reply.

"Don't understate that," Ihand-A said, quickly. "He tracked Gnok alone and unarmed through the jungle. All other members of the party, except Dr.Sey-Us, had been killed by Gnok in very unpleasant ways." Risc-Um felt embarrassed.

"I didn't do all that much," Risc-Um said, running his finger around the snug collar. He wasn't used to having his actions discussed in public and it made him as nervous as when he had first spoken with Ihand-A. The idea hit him and he turned the tables.

"You shouldn't be talking to us," Risc-Um said. "It was Sey-Us who brought Gnok down. While he blocked Gnok's path, we were making tracks for the boats and I mean fast tracks. Only Sey-Us and a few others had the guts to stand

192

and face the beast, tossing the bombs that knocked him out. We just sat in a boat and watched." It suddenly occurred to Sey-Us what Risc-Um was doing.

"Don't drag me into the story," Sey-Us said, wanting to keep the focus on his two stars. "Ihand-A's the real story. If it hadn't been for her we couldn't have gotten close to Gnok. He came to the village after her. She's really special to him." There were a few more questions before Sey-Us cut the reporters off.

"That's all for now. You'll be given all the details in the official press release."

"Will we be able to get some pictures of the beast, Dr. Sey-Us?" one of the photographers asked.

"Yes," Sey-Us replied. "I'm going to let you get some shots on stage after I make the introduction. You'll have the first photos for publication. You can get one of ihand-A standing in front of him."

"You missed your true profession, Dr. Sey-Us," one of them said. "You should have went into public relations."

"Those will be great shots," the nearest photographer said. Bending his head to Ihand-A, Risc-Um whispered to her.

"They don't realize that Sey-Us has been in public relations for years." She had to cover her mouth to hide the giggle that escaped.

"Answer one question, Dr. Sey-Us. Are you certain your big white beast is chained tight?" a reporter said. Sey-Us chuckled with a reassurance so strong it embarrassed the smart mouthed reporter. But Risc-Um knew Sey-Us' reassurance was overplayed.

"Come here," Sey-Us said, taking the reporter by the arm and leading him to where they could look out on stage. "Take a look for yourself."

They could see Gnok, now a slave who had once been a feared god. His shoulders was stooped in the steel cage and his wrists were chained to the top. His ankles were tangled in massive shains and anchored to great eyebolts in the cage floor. Only his head was free of any restraint. His blond hair was matted and his face dirty, which made his blue eyes stand out. But to Ihand-A, they were looking down in dispair.

Sey-Us told them Gnok had made no sound for many days. His hands were bound, not alowing him to thump on his chest. The reporter glanced at Sey-Us.

"I'll let the others go on stage first," the reporter said, stepping away from Sey-Us. "Let the eager ones have their fill while I maintain a conservative distance."

"Suit yourself," Sey-Us said, smiling. He turned back to Ihand-A and Risc-Um and they stepped to him.

"I want you to come on stage with me," Sey-Us said. "The curtain is about to go up." Ihand-A shuddered and backed away.

"I don't think I can stand being that close to him, Dr. Sey-Us." Sey-Us put an arm around her shoulders.

"There's nothing to worry about, my dear," he said, firmly, pulling her gently along with him. "We've taken a lot of spirit out of him since you last saw him. Gnok's virtually harmless now." Risc-Um wasn't about to take that at face value.

"That's what you believe," Risc-Um said. "No one can ask Gnok about that." He felt he knew Gnok better than Sey-Us did. Gnok turned into a harmless beast? Not very likely, Risc-Um thought.

Ihand-A pressed against Risc-Um's side as they stepped onto the stage. Gnok turned sad eyes to her, making the chains tinkle slightly, and watched every move she made.

The photographers began arranging their cameras and flash equipment.

"As soon as I get the shot of Ihand-A beside the beast, my paper will have it out in hours in a special edition," one photographer said, hoping to outdo his colleagues.

"Are you certain he can't get lose, Dr. Sey-Us?" A reporter asked, glancing apprehensively at Gnok. They all seemed to take a step back at the question.

"Of course he is," another reporter replied. "Dr. Sey-Us isn't going to take any chances." Sey-Us gave Ihand-A's arm a reassuring pat.

"You won't have to stay here long, Ihand-A," Sey-Us said. I'm going out, the curtain will rise, and I'll make a short speech. Then you and Risc-Um pose for the photographers, tell the audience what happened on the island and then leave. You and Risc-Um can go someplace quiet for dinner." Risc-Um was listening and thought Sey-Us was too sure of himself. The feeling Risc-Um had was telling a very different story.

Ihand-A was grateful that Sey-Us had pulled strings and had gotten her an apartment across from Risc-Um's and only a few blocks from the arena. Risc-Um didn't like staying at his parents' home when the ship was in port because his father disapproved of his chosen vocation.

Sey-Us went on stage and faced the audience as an air of anticipation built. His voice carried to the audience as the photographers waited impatiently. Ihand-A moved close to Risc-Um and he put an arm around her shoulder. Gnok saw this and his chains clanked feebly.

"Friends, distinguished colleagues, I am about to tell you a very strange, but true story," Sey-Us began. "A story no one could believe without proof. I've brought back living proof. A legend from the depths of the Forgotten Zone. My companions helped in the capture of a beast that existed before the dawn of our civilization. It was an incredible adventure for two of our party. A venture that cost the lives of ten of our party." The skeptical reporter tapped the person beside him.

"Ten of the ship's crew," he whispered. "He's not mentioning how many natives were killed by that beast. Lase-Um, who covers transportation and science, went aboard the No'mo and interviewed the crew. The real story was told by an old Chimp sailor named Pablae."

"My paper listed only eight of the crew killed," the reporter said. The skeptic shook his head.

"Sey-Us is sure devious," the skeptic said, in a low tone. Sey-Us had continued, enhancing certain points.

"Before I proceed further, I'm going to introduce the two most important persons of this amazing adventure," Sey-Us said, and motioned to Ihand-A and Risc-Um. "First, Ihand-A who was a captive of Gnok and Risc-Um who rescued her from under Gnok's very nose." As they walked onto the stage and stopped beside Sey-Us the audience applauded and they both bowed stiffly.

Now I will show you the most amazing thing you will ever see," Sey-Us said, and motioned for the curtain to be lifted. He was hamming it out in his best dramatic style. Risc-Um bent his head to Ihand-A.

"He's leaving it open in case he captures something bigger in the future," he whispered.

"He was a god on the island," Sey-Us continued. "Now he comes
to civilization as a captive. A specimen to satisfy our scientific curiosity. Friends, distinguished colleagues, behold Gnok, living god of a prehistoric island."

As the curtain rose, a murmur grew in the arena. The mood had abruptlu changed and it pleased Sey-Us to no end. Sey-Us stood in front of the cage flaunting his mastery

196

of the situation and this calmed the audience. Behind him, Gnok turned his head making the chains sound like he was trembling. Sey-Us reached for Ihand-A and pulled her reluctantly beside him.

"Allow me to introduce the bravest female I've ever called my permanent personal aide." The audience applauded and Sey-Us knew he was in control.

"Ihand-A lived through an experience no one could have dreamed of," Sey-Us continued.. "She was saved by the No'mo's fearless first mate, Risc-Um." Risc-Um stepped beside her and slipped his hand around hers. The audience was aware they were seeing romance and applauded again.

"Before we relate our amazing discoveries, the press will come on stage," Sey-Us said. "Friends, esteemed colleagues, you will witness the first photographs of Gnok taken in captivity." Gnok's chains continued their faint rattle as the photographers trooped out. Sey-Us pulled Risc-Um and Ihand-A closer to the cage. She tried to resist, pleading silently with her eyes.

"Don't worry," Sey-Us said, softly. That didn't help as she tried to control the cold fear pulsing through her. Sey-Us encouraged her with assuring whispers and she done her best in the distressing situation.

The flash units boiled as cameras clicked filling the stage with a dazzling blaze of light. Gnok curled his thick, fleshy lip up from his yellowed teeth and cut loose a blood-curdling roar. It was the first time since the island he had showed any of his former self. As his rumbling continued, the arena filled with an alarmed silence. Everyone seemed frozen, even Sey-Us, as a murmur of alarm ran through the audience. Risc-Um's expression became one of apprehension as Ihand-A tried to stifle a cry as she cringed against Risc-Um. Sey-Us helh up his hands.

"There's no reason to be alarmed," Sey-Us said, confidently. But Risc-Um noted a distinct trace of nervousness in his voice.

"Those chains are made of tempered carbon steel," Sey-Us said. It seemed he was right as Gnok's rumbling fell to a low muttering, but his chains were moving as if they were alive.

"Move closer to Ihand-A, Risc-Um," A photographer said. The scintillating flashes again filled the stage and Ihand-A turned away and covered her face. Risc-Um turned to Sey-Us while trying to shield Ihand-A from reporters.

"That's it, Sey-Us," Risc-Um said. "I'm taking Ihand-A away now." Risc-Um took hold of her arm and tried leading her past the photographers.

"Hold it, Risc-Um," Sey-Us commanded.

"Let's get another of you and Ihand-A a reporter said, more persistent than the others. The blaze flashed across the stage for the third time. Gnok's mouth opened and a roar came out like when he was free to do as he pleased. Risc-Um put an arm around Ihand-A as the beast-god began to struggle furiously, his rage building.

"Flaming hell!" Sey-Us whispered, as he turned to the cage. Risc-Um and Ihand-A were foremost in his mind as Sey-Us turned to the press and raised his arms.

"Stop the cameras," Sey-Us shouted. "He thinks you're attacking Ihand-A."

"Get away from her," Risc-Um said, pushing the photographers aside. Sey-Us stepped in quickly trying to get the photographers away from Ihand-A, but knew it was too late.

Gnok became quiet, pushed himself erect, and stood frighteningly straight. His head banged against the top of the cage and knocked it loose. He grasped the chain and pulled until great links began to bend until they snapped sounding like thunder in the arena. The bracelets, belt, and ankle chains were the only thing that held him. He took the belt and twisted until it fell away and he beat on his chest. He turned his attention to the eyebolts in the floor and wrenched them loose. His revived strength was turned to the bars of the cage, the only remaining barrier between him and Ihand-A.

Panic gripped the audience and it became a shrieking, brawling wave stopping for nothing. The civilized audience was reduced to clawing and beating at each other madly striving to get to the nearest exit. Risc-Um pulled Ihand-A along until they got to the exit. Behind them, they heard the bars moan as Gnok bent them until Gnok's roar filled the place with a challenge.

FINIS

Risc-Um opened the door of the car he had parked at the rear stage entrance and Ihand-A got in. He quickly got behind the wheel, started the engine, and drove away from the growing pandemonium. He kept an eye on the rearview mirror. Ihand-A was relieved to be away from Gnok.

"Where are we going, Risc-Um?" Her voice betrayed her fear.

"The University Dormatory Building. It's the highest place around here. We can wait on one of the upper floors until this is over, or Sey-Us gets things under control."

Before turning the corner, Risc-Um saw Gnok crash through the side of the arena into the light of the street. He raced along deserted, brightly-lit streets, turning down a dimly lit street. A few minutes later, Risc-Um stopped the car in front of slightly lit building. They got out of the car and went it.

"The elevator," Risc-Um said, leading Ihand-A toward it. His uneasy feeling was fading now that the worst had happened. The doors slid open and they stepped inside. When the doors closed, they breathed sighs of relief. The elevator stopped with a light jerk and the doors opened on the hallway of the dim tenth floor. They went along, Risc-Um trying each door until he found one unlocked. He pushed it open and they went in closing the door behind them.

Gnok drove through the wall and found himself in bright lights. He wanted to find Ihand-A and began seeking ger. A deputy stepped forward and emptied his revolver at Gnok and stared incredulously that it had no effect. Gnok simply stomped on him and moved away sniffing the air. He picked up her scent and moved in the direction of the Dormitory Building.

The room was furnished with two beds and chairs, and a desk with a lamp that Risc-Um turned on as Ihand-A sat down on the bed. Risc-Um went to the single window and looked down at the street below. It was empty and nobody was in sight.

"I don't think I can take much of this waiting, Risc-Um. It almost feels like being back on the island." He turned to her.

"We'll be safe here. Everything will work out." He used a calm tone hoping to get her to relax. He sat down beside her and put his arm around her. She pressed her face against him and shivered. He tried to comfort her with his embrace but he was growing edgy. His gut feeling had returned more strongly than before.

"Our troubles are over," he said, lifting her head from him. "It's Sey-Us' problem now." She trembled.

"I hope you're right," she said, unconvinced. "What if he follows us?"

"We were away from there before Gnok got out of his cage," Risc-Um said, trying to keep her calm.

The area around the arena was in turmoil. Deputies and fire fighting equipment were racing through the streets without knowing where they were going or what they were supposed to do. Sey-Us was in emergency talks with authorities about Gnok's quick recapture.

"Where could he have gone, Dr. Sey-Us?" the chief deputy asked, while other officials listened in silent alarm. "There hasn't been a confirmed sighting of that beast for the last half hour." Sey-Us gave him an annoyed look.

"Flaming hell! He has to be somewhere. He's too big to stay hidden for long." Annoyane broke into his lecture voice.

"Dr. Sey-Us, you know more about this animal than anyone," the mayor said. "Can you give us some idea of what he might do and where he might go?" Sey-Us didn't have to think about that.

"He'll be trying to find Ihand-A Risc-Um took her from the arena before I had a chance to ask where they would go." Sey-Us knew Ihand-A was the reason Gnok had escaped. He wanted her but why remained a mystery. A deputy had already checked both of their apartments and found them unoccupied.

Following his nose, Gnok was certain he would soon find his shining female. He had cuningly evaded his trackers by climbing a building and crossing the roofs. He stopped on a moderaly tall building and sniffed the air. He caught her scent and it seemed to be coming from a much taller building not far from where he was. He was certain that was where she was and determined to get her. But to do this, he would have to cross open ground. He would be stealthy enough not to be seen. Quickly and quietly, he went over the side of the building and set off for the Dormitory Building.

Ihand-A lay on the bed with her eyes closed as Risc-Um paced between the door and window, Always stopping to look out. Nothing below had changed in the deserted street. He could hear the whine of sirens in the direction of the arena and wondered how Sey-Us was handling the situation. Where they were seemed undisturbed and Risc-Um missed Gnok's approach. He was now wishing he had told Sey-Us where they were coming, but he hadn't known himself until they were on the way.

Risc-Um stopped at the window and became uneasy when he saw a number of deputy cars cautiously approaching the building. His stomach tightened in anticipation of imminenet action. A terrified scream from across the hall quickly distracted Risc-Um. He leaped for the door, opened it, and was across the hall to the origin of the scream. Opening the door, he found a wide-eyed female staring out the window. Risc-Um saw a huge wrist with a metal bracelet pass from view. The female fell over the bed in a dead faint as the sound of braking glass came from behind him.

Racing back into the room, Risc-Um saw Gnok's hand coming through the window. He grabbed a chair, lifted it over his head, and brought it down with all his strength. It shattered against Gnok's arm and the hand slammed him against the wall knocking him out.

Ihand-A lay in a faint as Gnok pulled the bed to the window. He picked her up and carefully lifted her through the window. He rumbled and cradled her in his arm with the same care he had used precviously and started down the building. Almost to the ground, two deputies fired at him with their revolvers. He roared at them and climbed for the roof.

When Risc-Um came around, he used the wall to get to his feet. He staggered to the window in time to see Gnok pass climbing for the top. He stuck his head out and saw the beast-god vanish over the parapet. Risc-Um knew there was no other place for Gnok to go. He began wondering how Gnok had found them. As he stepped into the hallway, a spell of dizziness overcame Risc-Um as he reeled toward the elevator.

On the ground floor, Risc-Um walked unsteadily from the elevator as fast as his throbbing head would allow. Outside he found the deserted street now coursing with movement. He began preparing himself for the grim task that lay ahead. Glancing up, he saw Gnok peek over the parapet and noticed there were no other buildings near enough for him to make an escape. There was only one way he could move – down.

From intersecting streets, deputy cars raced toward the building with sirens wailing loudly and uselessly as there wasn't any traffic. A few deputies stood by one car holding rifles sporting scopes. Risc-Um turned back into the building and a phone. He caught snatches of conversation from the deputies.

"How did that thing get loose?"

"I don't know. I do know those chains were strong enough to have held a ship in port." Risc-Um was more aware of Gnok's strength than they were. He also knew the imagined attack on Ihand-A had given him that unbelievable burst of energy.

"Fire coming from any other direction?" a deputy asked, looking up at the building.

"We're going to need laders to get up there," said another.

"There isn't a ladder in the city that will reach the top of that building," An officer deputy said.

Risc-Um had picked up the phone when Sey-Us pushed his way past the deputies and saw Risc-Um. He hurried to him.

"Where's Ihand-A?"

"He got her, Sey-Us. He went to the top and now he's trapped ." Risc-Um felt better now that Sey-Us had arrived.

"I don't understand how he was able to find us," Risc-Um said. "I didn't decide where to go until after we left the arena." Sey-Us had a theory about that.

"Her secent," Sey-Us said. "That's the only way he could have followed her."

"Well he climbed up this building as quick as anything I've ever seen," Risc-Um said. He noted the looks he got from the deputies. Jabbing his finger up, Risc-Um spoke in an aggravated tone.

"That beast can climb anything around here." It was then Sey-Us had an insight.

"Of course! The roofs was how he got away from the arena without being seen." It gave Sey-Us a new understanding of Gnok.

"That was how he eluded the patrols and made his way here unseen," Sey-Us said, then stood with clenched fists and spilled every profane word he could think of. He didn't like being made to look like a fool and that was what Gnok had done.

"Look up there!" A deputy shouted, and pulled his revolver from its holster. Gnok was glaring down from his high perch still holding Ihand-A in one arm. The deputy opened fire and Gnok slipped from sight.

"How are we going to get her away from him, Sey-Us?" Risc-Um asked, desperately trying to think of a plan. Sey-Us shook his head.

"We're going to need all the help we can get," Sey-Us replied, and turned to the ranking deputy.

"Deputy, make certain the area around this building remains clear of all nonessential persons," Sey-Us said, feeling helpless. "Our only advantage is that we have him trapped. Only we're down here."

The chief deputy arrived and began organizing the deputies into squads for patrol around the building. They didn't want Gnok slipping doiwn the reversa side and escaping again. Nothing more could be
done until some plan had been worked out.

"Will bullets kill that beast, Dr. Sey-Us?" the chief deputy asked. Sey-Us didn't want to hear that Gnok was going to be destroyed.

"If enough were delivered fast enough. But I prefer to take him alive, if possible." The chief deputy gave him an incredulous look.

"That's crazy! He's trapped on a building and we have no way to reach him."

"He's got Ihand-A," Risc-Um snapped. "You can't shoot until she's safe." He was anxious to get some sort of rescue underway as there was no telling what Gnok might do.

"Believe me," Risc-Um added. "The higher he is the more secure he feels. That's probably why he went up there." Sey-Us nodded.

"He didn't go up until two deputies shot at him," the chief deputy said.

"He thought they were after Ihand-A," Sey-Us said.

"We have no way of getting him down from there," the chief deputy said. "Short of starving him out." The chief deputy was considering the number of casualties storming the roof might cost.

"We've got to work out a plan, Dr. Sey-Us," the chief deputy said. "What do you recommend?" The reporters and crowd was being held a block away when a sudden clamor ran the crowd and many pointed. Gnok was again looking down at the increasing multitude. A depth fired and Gnok vanished. It happened too quickly for Risc-Um to see whether he still held Ihand-A.

The building was illuminated as searchlights arrived. It seemed impossible that Gnok could be up there and remain unseen. As the chief deputy, Risc-Um, and Sey-Us watched, Gnok swung over the parapet and started down. Two deputies opened fire cauing Gnok to quickly pull himself back over the parapet.

"I don't want anymore firing," Sey-Us exploded, angrily. "That may have been our only chance to get him alive." The chief deputy glared at Sey-Us then turned to the deputies.

"There's to be no more unauthorized firing as long as the female is exposed," the chief deputy said. "Pass that word to all deputies."

"I saw her on his arm," Risc-Um said, trying to dispell the anger between Sey-Us and the chief deputy.

"I'm going to send a couple of deputies up to look over the situation," the chief deputy said. "If they can get her away from him, perhaps concentrated rifle fire will drive him down." Sey-Us didn't like what he heard but had no alternative to suggest. Risc-Um was
concerned at the lack of thought in the plan. Sey-Us looked at the deputies and it was clear to him none of them wanted to go.

"That's no good," Sey-Us said, calmly. "They couldn't force him down and might get killed."

"Then how do you suggest we solve this problem, Doctor?" the chief deputy asked.

"There he is again," a deputy shouted. This time Gnok was only peeking over the parapet, not exposing himself.

"That proves he's intelligent," Sey-Us said, firmly. "That's why we must have him alive. We must study that prehistoric intelligence."

"Be sensible, Sey-Us," the chief deputy snapped. "There'a no way to take him alive unless he comes down." It was clear he was angered by Sey-Us' insistence on taking him alive.

"Whatever we do," Risc-Um said. "We have to think of Ihand-A first." He was soberly weighing her odds of survival and not liking them.

"If you start shooting up there," Risc-Um continued. "No one can be certain how he'll react."

"Flaming hell!" Sey-Us erupted. "There's one way we haven't considered, and it may be our only chance." Risc-

Um and the chief deputy regarded him expectantly. Sey-Us knew there was no other option.

"We can use vapor bombs," Sey-Us explained. "There's no danger to the crowd. Send a couple of deputiesto the No'mo and bring a case here. We can knock him out without risking anyone." He made Ihand-A his first priority, but getting Gnok alive was his second.

"If you succeed in knohing him out, how are you going to get him down from there?" the chief deputy asked. Risc-Um had a sudden idea that seemed to answer that question.

"Banana peels!" Risc-Um exclaimed. Sey-Us and the chief deputy turned their attention to him.

"We throw banana peels around the edge of the parapet and pop him with one or two vapor bombs.
When he staggers close to the edge he'll slip and down he'll come."

"That sounds reasonable," the chief deputy said.

"The fall will kill him," Sey-Us protested.

"Listen, Sey-Us, Gnok is a tough cutomer," Risc-Um said. "He'll come down on the trees, that will break his fall, he'll only be bruised." Sey-Us wasn't enthusiasic, but could suggest nothing else.

"You have anything to add, Dr. Sey-Us?" the chief deputy asked.
Sey-Us shook his head. The chief deputy turned away and began spouting orders.

"Call the sanitation department and have them get a load of banana peels over here fast."

"I'm going up," Risc-Um said, pulling off his collar. "I did this once before so I might as well try again. When I get to the roof, have everyone down here do what they can to distract Gnok. Maybe I'll get lucky and get Ihand-A."

"I'm coming with you," Sey-Us said. "I wasn't much help on the island, so I might be able to help now." Risc-

Um regarded him and nodded. The chief deputy selected several deputies armed with rifles to accompany them. None of them liked the idea but kept silent.

"Let me hjave one of those rifles," Risc-Um said. A deputy who hadn't been selected handed Risc-Um his. Risc-Um checked the load and slid the bolt back in place. The chief deputy was giving Risc-Um an uncertain look.

"Don't worry," Sey-Us said. "Risc-Um's one of the sharpest shots under pressure I've ever seen."

They were crowded into the elevator when it stopped on the top floor. They moved through the hallway toward the dark stairs leading to the roof. They went up until they found themselves in an enclosure that had the only door to the roof and a small window where they could look out over part of the roof. But the locked door was an unexpected delay. In a hurried whispered conversation, Sey-Us sent one of the deputies to get the key from the custodian.

On the roof, Gnok paced restlessly. Risc-Um saw Ihand-A lying close to the parapet with Gnok between. Risc-Um decided to see if he could get the window open. He pressed his hands against its top and pushed. The movement had been quiet but something caught Gnok's attention and he came to the window and looked in. The deputies cringed against the wall as Risc-Um and Sey-Us pressed tightly below the window. When Gnok saw nothing, he went back to the edge of the roof. Risc-Um took a quick peek and saw Ihand-A was lying between Gnok's feet, her gown torn and soiled.

Everything began to happen at once. The deputy arrived with the key, two deputies with the vapor bombs, and a Chimp announcing he had five crates of banana peels at the bottom of the stairs and wanted to know what to do with them. Risc-Um had to tell the deputies their part in the plan.

He fervently hoped it would work because he knew they wouldn't get a second chance. He ordered a crate of peels brought up and distributed to the deputies.

"When I open the door, slip out and move around dropping banana peels from the bags. Keep out of sight as long as possible. When Dr. Sey-Us and I step out with vapor bombs, show yourselves." Risc-Um emphasized the conditions for firing their weapons.

"Hold your fire until Ihand-A is clear of the beast." He knew their holding fire was the most crucial factor since he could tell all were tense at facing Gnok.

"After the first bomb explodes, you can open fire if you have to," Risc-Um said, firmly. "I doubt bullets will be effective but they will distract him. Let's move." The deputies slung their rifles, picked up the bags of peels, as Risc'Um carefully unlocked the door. Pushing it slightly open, he peeked out then opened it letting the deputies out. All but the last went unseen.

Gnok caught movement from the corner of his eye and was instantly on the unlucky deputy. It was unfortunate, but it left Ihand-A ungarded and gave Risc-Um the chance he had been hoping for. He raced to her as Sey-Us stepped between them and Gnok holding two bombs.

Gnok caught the deputy and flung him from the building. His feet now on the parapet, he thumped his chest and roared out his victory. In that instant, his fate was sealed. He turned back to Ihand-A and had one bomb after the other go off in his face and the deputies opened fire. The rifles flashed and cracked sending their small missiles at the beast. Ihand-A opened her eyes and cringed against Risc-Um when the firing erupted. He pressed her close as he watched the event unfold.

Sey-Us was certain he saw surprise on Gnok's face as he staggered back and the effects of the gas began taking

210

effect. Gnok saw blood trickling down his chest and wiped at it. He turned his eyes to Ihand-A then reached for her. He collapsed to his knees staring at her with a confused look. She pressed against Risc-Um, not wanting to watch what was happening to him.

Gnok began coughing up blood as he pushed himself to his feet and growled at his small adversaries. The growl broke in a harsh, sundering cough, and he stood his full height and beat on his chest. His action seemed almost dignified to Sey-Us. The deputies had reloaded and resumed firing. The impact of so many bullets, combined with the accelerating action of the gas, staggered him toward the parapet. He climbed on the parapet and stood swaying. With strength ebbing he made a desperate leap that took him to the far parapet where his feet lost traction on the peels. His arms began flailing, he grabbed two deputies as he went over the parapet headfirst.

For an instant, high above the civilization that had consumed him, Gnok was in the majestic loneliness he had known on his mountaintop. Then he plunged to his death, imposed by his conquerers.

"Are you all right, Ihabd-A?" Risc-Um asked, in the heavy silence. She was trembling in an emotional mixture of thankfulness and sorrow. She looked at Risc-Um and tried to control herself.

"I'm all right."

"You don't have to worry about Gnok anymore," Risc-Um said, as unemotionally as he could.

Sey-Us and the remaining deputies leaned over the parapet. Sey-Us was full of mixed emotions as this final encounter had torn something loose in him.

"That was really something," one of the deputies said. "I was worried we might not be able to kill him."

"We didn't kill," Sey-Us said, coming to an understanding of Gnok.

"What do you mean?" asked the deputy next to him. Sey-Us turned a sad look on the deputy.

"It was emotion. As always, emotion wins over common sense and instinct. That's what killed him." Looking back down at Gnok's body, Sey-Us shook his head.

"I wish scientific advancement was a little less costly." He made a suspicious wipe at his eye. Turned, and walked from the parapet.

"Crazy as hell," the deputy mumbled as Sey-Us went through the door. He turned to the deputy next to him and shook his head.

"I'll never understand crack-brained scientists," the deputy said.

This concludes the report of the events that have delayed contact with the inhabitants of Ephus. Any further action regarding contact will be suspended until the council makes its decision. This ship will standby should the council decide to proceed with a contact party. It is the recommendation of the commander that contact be postponed until this civilization is more scientifically advanced.
END REPORT.

THE END